HQ110024

F

UK
CUSTOMER
SERVICE
EXCELLENCE
The Government Standard

GOD'S BOAT

Kaori Ekuni

Translated by Chikako Kobayashi

THAMES RIVER PRESS

God's Boat

THAMES RIVER PRESS
An imprint of Wimbledon Publishing Company Limited (WPC)
Another imprint of WPC is Anthem Press (www.anthempress.com)

First published in the United Kingdom in 2012 by
THAMES RIVER PRESS
75-76 Blackfriars Road
London SE1 8HA

www.thamesriverpress.com

Original title: Kamisama no boto
Copyright © Kaori Ekuni 1999
Originally published in Japan by SHINCHOSHA, Tokyo
English translation copyright © Chikako Kobayashi 2012

A CIP record for this book is available from the British Library.

ISBN 978-0-85728-249-1

Cover design by Laura Carless.

This title is also available as an eBook.

This book has been selected by the Japanese Literature Publishing Project (JLPP),
an initiative of the Agency for Cultural Affairs of Japan.

CONTENTS

TAKAHAGI, 1997

Mum tells me that when I was conceived, she and Dad were staying at a cottage resort on an island in the Mediterranean. It was a sunny, windless day, and the two of them were reading by the pool. Mum's book was a thick mystery novel, and Dad's was a collection of short stories. Mum says Dad drove her crazy because he'd start talking to her every time he finished one of his stories.

Mum was drinking a cocktail called a Sicilian Kiss. It was Dad's job to make the cocktails, and according to Mum, his Sicilian Kisses were "absolutely addictive" and "sweet enough to knock anybody out." She says that no other drink was as blissfully perfect for an afternoon outside as that luscious, amber-coloured drink. The ice in her glass sparkled in the sun. And as they read, Dad planted kisses on Mum's neck again and again. Mum felt like she was going to melt everywhere he kissed her, his lips were so hot. She says his lips were always like that.

It was quiet, there was no one around, the sky was brilliantly clear, and they hadn't a worry in the world.

When Dad pressed his lips against Mum's neck for a particularly long kiss, she let out a sigh in spite of herself and finally put her book down. Mum cradled Dad's head, and Dad put his arms around Mum's hips, wrapped his legs around hers, and squeezed her tight. Still entangled, they got up, went inside, and collapsed onto the bed.

"I'd just finished half of my third Sicilian Kiss," Mum says every time she tells the story.

You can't trust a lot of what Mum says, but I believe this story. I don't know why, but I feel like I remember the scene by the pool that sunny afternoon, the coolness of the air inside the room, and how the window just above the bed was ajar.

✦ ✦ ✦

The sand on the beach here is white. The beach probably gets crowded at some point in the summer, but at this time of year there's no one else around. What it comes down to is that there just aren't many people living here. Apparently, everyone knows everyone. I bend down and fill my hand with sand. There are lots of clear, salt-like granules. I let the sand fall through my fingers, stand back up, and start walking again. It's been two months since we moved to this town, and every day has been cloudy.

Yesterday I had a meeting with Soko's class teacher. She said that Soko was an excellent student.

"She's a very bright child."

"Thank you," I said. Cream-coloured curtains hung by the windows, and in front of them stood a row of shelves. The fluorescent lights were on even though it was the middle of the day. They gave off a hollow glow. It seemed kind of comical, the two of us facing each other, seated on either side of a desk in the centre of the empty classroom.

"I think it's because she's still new to this school," the teacher said, a practised smile appearing on her beige-painted lips. "But I've noticed that your daughter has a tendency to retreat into her shell."

"Her shell?" I asked, puzzled. She's not a bird, for god's sake.

The teacher nodded in all seriousness.

"Yes. But I don't think it's anything to worry about. She's probably still nervous about being at a new school."

I nodded. "May I smoke?"

"No, not here." The teacher looked embarrassed.

"Oh, I'm sorry."

Soko, nervous? I wondered, as I stared at the chalkboard. I wasn't surprised. I'd been nervous ever since I stepped into the classroom, too.

On the chalkboard it said:

Wednesday, 19th November
Today's class monitors: Takei & Kakuta.

I stride down the beach, shuffling my chestnut-coloured skirt this way and that. It's windy. The CD Walkman I borrowed from Soko looks like a cheap plastic toy, but I can hear Rod Stewart's husky voice just fine. I hum along to the song pouring from the earphones. The November ocean. The smell of the afternoon tide. I hum along to Rod Stewart, my guardian angel. I grab a stick lying by my feet and throw it into the distance.

The people who live in our block of flats are all a bit strange. The landlord wears odd-looking, dark-rimmed glasses and strikes me as someone who's not easily humoured.

Today the surf is high again. You could say I moved here for the waves. There's absolutely nothing in this town except for a rather grand hotel run by the local government, and a country club. The waves in this area are amazing, though – the way they crash and shatter into tiny white droplets.

Water is plentiful here. It trickles from springs on the street here and there, making faint gurgling sounds.

I like walking.

Maybe it's because of the fairy tales I heard as a child, but I always feel like I'm lost in a forest, wandering blindly in circles. Maybe I find comfort in walking because it brings me closer to that feeling.

I scramble up a boulder at the end of the beach. My brown suede flats are all worn out (they're threadbare where my little toes rub against them), and are moulded to me like they're a part of my feet. Through the soles I can feel the sharp – more so than rocky – edges of the rock beneath me. I take in the sound of waves, the salty wind.

I give myself an hour for my walks, but two or three hours pass easily if I'm not careful. It's always been this way.

"I was worried about you," the Professor often chided me.

"Have you ever given any thought to how you look when you're standing there like that, watching the cars go by?" he once said, his eyebrows lowered. He'd come looking for me when I'd been out for a while on one of my walks. "You look like you're possessed, like you're about to jump to your death."

I used to stand on footbridges a lot back then.

"Jump? Why in the world would I do that?"

"How should I know?" The Professor was tall and skinny, and his greying hair was quickly receding.

We always went home holding hands.

A close friend of my cousin made me a sign that says PIANO LESSONS. It's light pink with an illustration of piano keys at the bottom. The letters and keys are dark navy. It's pretty classy, and I like it.

I don't own much. There's the piano, the sign, an overnight bag's worth of clothes, and an espresso maker.

The Professor got me the espresso maker. At the time, all the espresso makers available in Japan were huge, industrial models. He'd found a small one for me in Europe somewhere.

It's been nine years since I left him. That means Soko is almost ten.

I have to start heading back. I try to be at home as often as I can in the afternoons, when Soko gets home from school. In my planner – my planner, decorated with a photo sticker of Soko and me – there's a slip of paper indicating what time Soko gets out of school each day of the week:

Monday	3:10
Tuesday	4:30 (gardening club)
Wednesday	2:10
Thursday	3:10
Friday	3:10
Saturday	12:10 (every other week)

Soko comes straight home for the most part, except on days she has cleaning duty, in which case she can be a few minutes late.

When I get home, Mum's reading a book with her feet soaking in a bucket of hot water. It's something she does often to warm up, because her hands and feet are always cold.

"Hi, honey," she says when she sees me.

"Hi, Mum."

I put down my bags – my schoolbag and a cream-coloured tote with an embroidered donkey and wheelbarrow full of flowers one of our neighbours in Soka, an old lady, made for me – and look at Mum's book.

"What are you reading?"

Mum shows me the cover.

"*The Sound of the Piano*," I read the title out loud. "Is it about pianos?"

"No, it's a novel."

Mum has really short hair. It's apparently the same hairstyle as this actress named Giulietta Masina. My hair is chopped straight across two inches below my shoulders. It's thin and lies flat, just like Mum's. Sometimes Mum says with disappointment, "If only your hair had been like your dad's," and gently strokes it. Dad's hair is supposedly very healthy, dark and thick with a slight wave. According to Mum, I have my dad's spine. A straight and beautiful spine. You can tell just by touching it, she says.

"Oh, by the way, thanks for this," Mum says, as she hands me my CD Walkman. I'd lent it to her this morning. I change schools a lot, which means I get a lot of going-away presents. Yu, Mayumi, and Chiyomi gave me the Walkman when I moved from Soka. In return, I gave them each a pencil with a plastic cat at the end. Mum tells me I should write to my friends. Letters, she says, make it to their destination anywhere in Japan for just eighty yen – no matter where we live. But I don't like writing letters that much. Writing a letter means having to wait for a reply, and I don't like waiting, because I'm afraid my friends might not write back.

The elementary school I go to now is my third. Behind the school there's a pile of tyres that we can play on. The tyres are my favourite thing about this school.

I began travelling when I was six months old. Well, to be exact, Mum was the one who began travelling, and she just took me with her.

"Ooh, chocolate," I say, noticing a box on the kitchen table. "Is it from Mr Ichijo?"

"Yep," Mum says, and nods. "He apparently got them in Kobe on a business trip."

"Hm."

Mr Ichijo is a customer at Daisy, the bar where Mum works, and a big fan of hers. Wherever we go, Mum wins over two or three customers within about a month. Mum laughs and says it's like a game played according to the rules, but some of her admirers are pretty serious about her. For Mum, though, it's just part of the job.

"You can have some chocolate after you've washed your hands."

Mum teaches piano at home during the day and works at Daisy at night. Teaching piano isn't enough to make a living. After all, she only has two students at the moment, a retired man and a thirteen-year-old girl. They both come once a week in the morning.

I'm allowed to play the piano whenever I want, and Mum will play anything I ask her to, but she doesn't give me lessons. She says that I have to find a different teacher if I'm going to take lessons, but I don't want to learn from someone else. I like the way Mum plays, especially Bach.

Late in the afternoon, I do my homework while Mum plays the piano beside me. We can see a small river and the village shop from our window. There's really not much going on in this town. I wonder how long we'll stay.

For dinner, we have roasted chicken with steamed vegetables. After I finish everything on my plate, Mum lets me have a glass of fruit-flavored milk. Mum's picky about what I eat.

I see Mum off when she leaves for work, and draw for a while after washing the dishes. I always use my black and white crayons the most. Just when I'd finished drawing a flower, a zebra, and a gazelle, the lady next door brings over some persimmons.

"You're such a good girl, always looking after yourself."

The lady sometimes brings fruit and other kinds of food for dinner, but I know what she's actually doing is checking up on me.

"Remember to lock up, okay?" she says, and casts a sharp glance at the stove.

"She's just a worrywart," Mum once said. "She's not a bad person."

"Isn't it rude, though, what she does?" I said, and Mum thought about it.

"Give her a break," she said. "But make sure you put the food she brings straight into the fridge. I don't want you eating any of it, just in case there's old tofu in it or something."

I eat a slice of persimmon and put the rest in the fridge.

I'm used to being alone at night, because that's when Mum usually works. There was just one town where she only worked during the day. But that's already in the box.

In the box is an expression Mum and I use when we're talking about something that's in the past. The good times never come back once they're in the past.

"But it's nothing to be sad about," Mum had said. She was wearing a colourful floral skirt. "Because what has happened will never change. It will always be. The things in the past are the only things that really belong to us."

That was what she said four years ago when I cried and complained about having to move. It was the first town in which I'd managed to make friends.

"Everything that has passed goes in the box, so we never have to worry about losing any of it. Isn't that lovely?"

I sometimes try to imagine what the box looks like, its shape, how big it is, what kind of lid it has, and what colour it is. In my head, the box has a fancy floral pattern just like the skirt Mum wore that day.

I usually go to bed at ten. I take a bath, brush my teeth, and lay out my futon – on my own, of course – as well as Mum's. I turn off the radio, which I keep on until bedtime, set the alarm for seven, and all three of us get under the covers. That's me, Allie, and the pink bear. The pink bear doesn't have a name. Allie is a white cyborg about four inches tall and made of rubber, with a machine gun in her right hand and a shield in the left. Mum won Allie for me at an arcade a long time ago. We've been sleeping together for years and years.

We sometimes spot-switch.

Spot-switching is a game that I invented. I set the alarm to go off every hour or two and go to sleep. Every time it rings, we get up and switch spots. Let's say we start off with Allie on the left, me in the middle, and the pink bear on the right. In the first spot-switch, I move to the left, the pink bear goes in the middle, and Allie goes on the right. The next time the alarm goes off, it's the pink bear on the left, Allie, and then me. And we just keep going and going. Mum joins us, too, on her days off. Spot-switching is a lot more fun with four people. We can use two sets of futons when it's the four of us, which means that whoever's on one end is really far away from whoever's on the other end.

Of all the places we've lived, Imaichi was my favorite. We lived on the second floor of a public bathhouse. That was where I learned the colour of sunlight, came to know what the bathhouse windows looked like first thing in the morning, the colour of hot water, the smell of steam.

The Suzuki school probably had something to do with it, too. With what our lives were like.

The Suzuki school is a piano school, and that's where Mum taught full time, giving piano and voice lessons. That means she didn't have to work at night. As far as I can remember, our eight-month stint in Imaichi was the only time Mum didn't work at night.

I wake up every morning at seven. Mum goes to bed late so she's still fast asleep then. For breakfast I always have cereal and eggs, which I make myself. My favourite is soft-boiled eggs – but most of the time I make scrambled eggs, or sunny-side up.

Today, I fry my eggs sunny-side up. The yolks don't break when I slide the eggs onto my plate, and take that as a sign that the day's off to a good start. We're using the climbing pole – which I'm really bad at – in P.E. today, so I'm desperate for good omens. It's unusually sunny this morning in Takahagi, which Mum says is "always cloudy, like Amiens." Amiens is a small town in northern France, and if what Mum says is true, it's cloudy there all year round.

I pour soy sauce on my eggs. I think the good thing about having eggs sunny-side up is that they go well with a lot of different condiments. I'm usually a salt person, but when we have spinach sautéed in butter with our eggs (which happens only on weekends, when Mum makes breakfast), I sprinkle steak sauce on them. Other days, like today, I have my eggs with soy sauce.

The sun pours through the kitchen window, giving the silver metal of the sink a whitish glow. Water leaks from the tap, not with a drip-drip-drip, but with a sudden irregular series of splashes. This is what mornings are like for Mum and me, and our house.

After I finish eating, I take my plate to the sink, brush my teeth, and put on my socks. Once I'm all ready, I'm supposed to go say good-bye to Mum. She'll stick both arms out from under the covers and stroke my hair. Then she'll cradle my head and say good-bye groggily, her voice hoarse.

But today I'm not ready to say good-bye at the usual time. I can't find the socks I was planning to wear. I empty all my drawers looking for them. Not just the sock drawer, but the other ones, too. I look in the laundry basket and the washing machine. I also search through Mum's drawers in case they've got mixed up. Hers are big drawers that rattle when I pull them open.

"What are you doing?" By the time Mum calls out from her futon, the room is a complete mess.

"I can't find my socks," I tell her, because I have no other choice. "The white ones with the lacy thing at the top. With the really thin navy blue trim."

"Just wear something else," Mum says, sticking an arm out from under the covers and waving it dismissively.

"But those are the ones I want to wear today," I insist. The trousers I'm wearing are on the short side, and my ankles show when I walk. It suddenly occurs to me to check the veranda, but there's nothing on the pink clothesline.

"Fine."

Mum gets up and throws on a thick cardigan she keeps draped on her futon. She has a really dull, unhealthy complexion in the mornings.

"Brrr." She quickly puts on some socks and rubs her face with her hand. "So you're looking for the white socks with the lacy thing at the top, right?"

Mum pokes around for my socks in all the places I've already looked. The drawers, the laundry basket, the veranda. I usually leave the house at five past eight, and it's already quarter past.

"White and lacy, white and lacy…" Mum repeats like a magic spell. It's dark in the bedroom, with all the windows and sliding doors still shut. Watching her as she looks for the missing socks, I get sad.

"Don't worry. I'll wear something else." I pick out a pair of light blue socks.

"No, just wait. There's no reason why they shouldn't be here," Mum says, but I put on my other socks and my backpack and grab the tote the old lady in Soka gave me.

"I'm going to be late."

Mum looks at me and raises her eyebrows, as if she's given up. Suit yourself, her expression says.

"Bye." I put on my sneakers. A clay sculpture I made in second grade sits on top of the shoe cupboard by the front door.

"Bye." Standing in the doorway, Mum looks cold and folds her arms in front of her chest. She squints as I open the door. "Great weather."

"Yeah."

The air outside is crisp.

"Have a good day," Mum says, as always.

"You too, Mum," I say, and close the door. The lady from next door is taking the rubbish out.

It's Thursday. That means we're climbing poles in P.E.

Mum later found my socks behind the washing machine.

FIRST SNOW

I cycle to work. Having grown up in Tokyo, I've often been stumped by the quiet and impenetrability of all the other cities I've been to in my nine years of travelling. But when it comes to cycling, it's so much better away from Tokyo, where there are fewer people and cars, and bigger roads, and where the wind actually carries the scent of the grass and the trees. I especially like cycling home. It's always the dead of night, and not a single soul is out. The stars are frozen in the night sky, and I ride home in the dark with my scarf fluttering in the wind. Sometimes I stand on the pedals like a teenage boy and pump as fast as I can.

Daisy is a small bar, and in addition to the female owner and the bartender, another girl, Maho, works there. I'm thirty-five and Maho's twenty-nine, but naturally, at Daisy, we both pretend we're a bit younger than we really are.

It's a comfortable place to work. It's nothing to brag about, but at all of the places I've worked, I've never caused any trouble or had to leave prematurely – that is, before leaving the city itself.

According to the Professor, though, not sticking out like a sore thumb and blending in are two totally different things.

"You don't ever settle into a place, do you?" he'd often say. I don't stand out, but I don't adapt to my surroundings. It's not a bad thing, but apparently it makes those around me feel very alone.

There's one thing I'm confident in.

It's a skill for which I'm highly valued everywhere I work, more than for any talent I might have for entertaining customers. I'm great at cleaning, and I'm especially proud of the care and efficiency with which I can wipe things down with a cloth. For example, I'll flip over the heavy round stools in the bar and wipe the backs carefully, one by one. Usually no one wants to be the first to go inside on the day after we've smoked out the cockroaches, but on such days I'm filled with an emotion not unlike hope or a thirst for a challenge, and arrive at work more motivated than usual.

We're open until two, but we're rather laid back about customers taking their time and sometimes don't close until three. Then there are days when we've got nothing to do after our last customers have left around twelve.

After we close up, Maho and I usually have a cup of coffee before going home. We find that it refreshes us and helps us shift gears before we go back to our respective homes.

Maho lives with her boyfriend.

"I have the great honour of supporting him financially," she said one day, laughing. She's a pretty girl and wears a delicate gold chain on her left wrist, which she says was a gift from her boyfriend.

"I eloped when I was seventeen," she tells me today. "I made my parents cry a lot."

When Maho laughs, she cocks her head slightly to the side.

We drink instant coffee, and I make mine really strong. Maho likes hers weaker and adds a little bit of milk and sugar.

"What about your parents, Yoko?" Maho asks, and now I cock my head.

"I don't know. I haven't seen them in a long time."

"Really?" That's the only thing Maho says, and she smiles at me gently with compassion.

I bike into the wind. Towards home, where Soko waits.

When I get home, I find Soko asleep under the covers with her two dolls, as usual. I'm entranced by her sleeping face, and can't stop myself from lying down beside her. I feel the slightly damp air given off by a sleeping child. Caressing Soko's forehead, I'm startled by the coldness of my fingertips. Still, Soko is a deep sleeper and doesn't stir one bit, taking quiet, even breaths. I brush back Soko's fringe with my icy fingers over and over again. Her forehead feels exactly like his.

At times like this, I feel as though time has stopped. As if Soko and I are going to be trapped inside the night forever. The night is long. It feels like it'll never end, quiet enough to swallow anything and everything. That's how it's always felt to me. And it's not that I dislike the night. When I was living with the Professor, I always stayed up late while he went to bed early.

Soko was born at night, too, near the break of dawn. I was in a hospital room with four beds, two of them empty. The tiny enclosed space between the white curtain and the wall was quiet, clean, and comfortable, oddly enough. I could see the parking lot below, outside the window. There was a partially-read book and a cup of ice water by my bedside.

My contractions grew more frequent, the way they were supposed to. I was alone.

I knew the Professor was waiting at home, wide awake. I knew he would be anxious, trying to reorganise his bookshelf and giving up, letting the tea he'd carefully brewed go cold untouched and making another pot. But still, I was alone. The night seemed endless.

Whenever I drifted off between my contractions, I dreamt about my true love, over and over again. In my dreams, he was smiling.

What a beautifully shaped forehead.

That was what I thought every time he appeared. Over and over again.

Soko was born at 3.50am. She was a small baby and cried feebly, but she was just spared the incubator.

It was a moonless night in May, and only the stars shone brightly. Above the parking lot, on the other side of the window with the small white curtains.

Soko stirs under the covers.

"Mum?" she says, opening her eyes slightly.

"Sorry, I woke you," I say, and drape myself on top of her. "Were you scared without me?"

Soko wraps her arms around my neck and says, "No, Allie's here, so I was fine."

I smile at the tiny doll by my daughter's head. "Oh, that's right."

Allie is a rubber cyborg, imposingly armed with what looks like a jet engine on her back.

By the time Soko unclasps her arms from my neck she's already asleep, her breath slow and even. Her tiny nails are painted light pink. It's probably magic marker. Pulling the covers over her shoulders, I get up to take off my make-up in the bathroom.

◆ ◆ ◆

Rikako and I grew close during P.E. Neither of us is very good at the climbing pole. The pole is just inside the school gates, to the left, in the corner of the school grounds farthest from the classrooms.

"Do you think it's because my arms aren't strong enough?" I say, and Rikako furrows her brows, observing the boys as they climb.

"I think it's all about the strength in the palms of your hands and the backs of your feet," she says. Rikako's hair's in a bob, and she has a Myu key chain on her bag.

Every day after lunch, we run out to the playground behind the classrooms to ride the seesaw. There are also tyres we can play on, an incinerator, and a field of clovers. For some reason I've always liked playgrounds behind school buildings, and find myself playing behind schools wherever I move.

"So it's just you and your mum," Rikako says as we go up and down on the seesaw. "Do you have any pets?"

"Nope."

Going up on a seesaw is so much more fun than coming down. You kick the ground to go up, but you come down without doing anything.

"Hmm. We have a cat."

I love it when the seesaw shoots up and my bum flies into the air at the top for just a split second.

"What's its name?"

"Goo," Rikako says.

"Goo?"

"Yeah. Goo."

What a weird name, I think to myself. Her dad came up with it, she says.

I kick the ground. The seesaw and I soar upward. The moment Rikako reaches the ground, the seesaw comes to a jerky stop, and my bum is thrown off the seat just a tiny bit. Seesawing is best on cloudy days.

The bell rings. Bells at all schools sound kind of silly.

"Can I come over sometime?" Rikako asks, as we climb off.

When I get home from school, Mum is playing the piano. It's the 'Forty-Eight.' You can hear the piano from outside our flat, and plus, Mum plays so powerfully that I can tell it's her right away.

"Hi, Mum." I put my bags down, wash my hands, and gargle.

"Hi, honey."

Still sitting in front of the piano, Mum hugs me and presses her cheek against mine. "You're cold," she says with a smile.

"Oh, wait, I have a letter from school." I dig around in my bag. Mum gets really annoyed when I forget to show her notices from school and tests that have been corrected and handed back.

"Anything interesting happen at school today?" Mum asks, lighting a cigarette and getting up to make coffee in the kitchen.

"Not really."

I hand her the note and take a piece of chocolate from the table. Mum probably got the chocolate as a gift from a customer again. Mum says she gets all her nutrients from cigarettes, coffee, and chocolate.

"A school ski trip?!" Mum shrieks, and falls silent. I brace myself.

"No way. There's no way I'm letting you go." Mum's expression is stiff. "It's too dangerous. Please don't go."

I swallow my chocolate and slowly, carefully, try to explain.

"We're going to have ski instructors. And our teachers will be there with us, of course, and…"

"No. There's absolutely no way I'm letting you go," Mum cuts in. She squeezes me for one, two, three, four, five seconds, a long time. I can smell a mix of shampoo, cigarettes, and perfume. Mum's scent.

"Okay, I get it." I say, still wrapped in Mum's arms, giving up. "Let go. I promise I won't go on the trip."

Mum hugs me tight one more time, and finally lets go. Her eyes are bloodshot, and her nose is red. Mum cries easily and when her nose gets red, I can tell she's about to cry.

"I'm sorry," Mum says, looking like a child who's just been scolded.

"It's okay. It's not like I wanted to go that badly, anyway," I say, and look at the cigarette between Mum's fingers. Things like this happen sometimes when you're living with my mum. "Mum, you're dropping ashes."

She looks at the cigarette in her hand, then the floor, and says softly, "It doesn't matter." The espresso maker is making bubbling noises.

✦ ✦ ✦

"But you don't really believe that, do you?" Maho asks, her tiny bottom on a stool, which she swivels in half circles. She's wearing a zebra-print miniskirt and high heels that look like they could pierce the floor. "You don't seriously believe that you'll be reunited with some guy who disappeared ten years ago, do you?"

We put up the Christmas tree today at Daisy. It's a small, fake tree.

I take a sip of coffee and give her a smile instead of an answer. Maho lifts her thin eyebrows high to look shocked, but it's obvious that she's not the least bit surprised. With her chin resting on one hand, elbow on the counter, she lights a slim menthol cigarette. The tales we share with each other here are just that, and tales shouldn't be received with shock or disgust.

"What are we going to do with you?" Maho says, blowing a straight stream of smoke from her pursed, shapely lips. There's a small teddy bear on one of her long nails. A light brown teddy bear with a red ribbon around its neck.

"Cute, isn't it?" she says brightly when she notices I'm staring at it. "It's a sticker." She opens the small bag on her lap and takes out another one. "Do you want one, too?"

I smile and shake my head. "I'll pass." My hands are for playing the piano, so I keep my nails clipped short. Plus, I've got clunky fingers with big joints.

"Actually, could I have one?" I ask, suddenly remembering Soko's pink magic-markered nails.

The next day, I feel under the weather and decide to read at home instead of going for a walk in the afternoon. I've reread the paperback with the yellow cover so many times that the cover is pretty tattered. Soko's father gave it to me a long time ago.

From now on, I'm only going to use my head for wearing hats. It makes me sad every time I reach that line uttered by the book's main character.

Maho might think I'm being ridiculous, but I've never doubted him.

He promised he would find me. "Wherever you are, whatever you're doing, I swear I will find you again," he said.

Anyone who saw the look in his eyes when he said those words would know. They'd know they had to believe him. Even if his promise is never realized, I won't doubt him for as long as I live.

✦ ✦ ✦

Mum was coughing all through the night yesterday. It kept her from getting much sleep, and she's already up drinking coffee when I wake up. She says she doesn't have a fever but that her stomach is sore from all the coughing.

"I didn't know I even had stomach muscles," Mum says sullenly.

Still, Mum cuts up an apple to serve with breakfast. "It's not often that I'm up so early," she says as she peels the fruit. She makes the apple pieces look like bunnies, with the peel in small v-shaped rabbit ears.

"Do you get nervous when you go to a new school?" Rikako asks, sitting on the other side of the seesaw, her underwear peeking from the navy blue woollen skirt she's wearing today.

"Not so much," I lie. I get outrageously nervous when I go to a new school. I get so scared that I can barely fall asleep the night before my first day and can't eat in the morning. The playground, shoe lockers, hallways, and teachers' offices all make me feel that I won't fit in. What I hate most are the posters on the walls that say things like "Use soap when washing your hands," or "No running in the halls." They make me feel like a complete outsider.

"Hmm." Rikako says, and looks away.

Whenever I start a new school, I tell myself that I don't have to fit in, and that I don't have to make any friends. If I remind myself of this over and over again, I begin to believe it and can relax. That way, I can make myself go to any new school.

The playground behind the school building is covered in shade. It's especially shady by the edges of the building. The air there is cool and moist, and there's grass and moss on the ground. When the bell rings five minutes before class and everyone heads back to the classrooms, I stand alone with my back against the building and close my eyes. I breathe in deeply – the smell of dirt and the white, rough wall of the building. Just for a little bit.

Then I run inside to get back to my classroom on time.

"Why do we have to move all the time?" I once asked. It was when we were leaving Soka. I was only six years old and it was already my sixth move. The first two moves I don't remember, because I was still a baby.

"Do you not like moving?" Mum asked me. She was sitting in front of the piano with a pencil in her right hand and a cigarette in her left. Still holding them, she sat me on her lap. "Why, have you grown fond of this place?"

I was silent. I didn't know what it was that I didn't want or what it was that I did. "Why?" I asked again, because I didn't know what else to say. "Why do we move all the time?"

Mum pressed her lips against my hair again and again. "Because we got on God's boat."

"God's boat?" I asked, but Mum didn't explain it to me any further. "Yes, God's boat."

She picked me off her lap, and that was the end of our conversation.

On the first Monday of December, Mum and I celebrate Dad's birthday. Mum usually doesn't drink, but every year on this day only, she drinks red wine. I have a sip, too. Mum plays the piano and we sing 'Happy Birthday'.

We celebrate four birthdays every year. Mum's, mine, Dad's, and the Professor's. The Professor is Mum's ex-husband. He was a teacher at a music college with a quiet, gentle smile and "played Bach with incredible precision," says Mum. He was a father to me for six months, from the time I was born until Mum and I left on our journey.

"Come here. Let's take a picture," Mum says, and I stand in front of her, where she's sitting. We snuggle up against each other and stare at the camera lens, waiting for the self-timer to go off. There's the buzz, the blinking light, the sound of the shutter being released – a sound so final – and a flash goes off at precisely the same moment. Our smiles have been captured.

Mum always takes a picture of me on Dad's birthday. She says someday she's going to show Dad the pictures of me getting bigger every year and of her looking not a day older (her own words, of course).

I think about Dad. There isn't much I know about him. All I know are his name and birthday, his height and weight ten years ago, the fact that he has healthy, dark, thick hair with a slight wave, that his bone structure looks like mine (or that mine looks like his?), that he's good at making cocktails, and that he looks "incredibly sexy" after two days without shaving. And not one of these things have I confirmed for myself.

The roast beef covered in onions that Mum makes for Dad's birthday every year is delicious, but to be honest, I don't like the day very much. I like my birthday, Mum's, and the Professor's better.

"Do you want cake?" Mum asks as she kisses me on the cheek.

"Yes!" I answer, and go to the kitchen for plates. The English-language weather forecast is on the radio.

I don't know why, but Dad's birthday makes me a little sad every year. Maybe because that's how Mum looks.

✦ ✦ ✦

The Professor wasn't surprised at all when I told him I wanted a divorce.

"I'm sorry," he said. That was it. I shouldn't have told him about Soko. I shouldn't have told him that I would soon be giving birth. Of course, it was too late.

I drink the rest of the wine alone as I watch Soko sleep. Today is my true love's birthday.

Long ago, he and I often drank together. He drank with such grace no matter what he was drinking, quietly and smoothly pouring the liquid into his body. I used to imagine the liquid flowing down his throat and chest and dropping straight into his stomach. Once inside his body, the alcohol would be converted into whatever nutrients his body needed. I was convinced of this; the way he drank it could only be so.

We even drank during the day in the back of his music store. The store, which for the most part carried guitars, was so narrow it was like a hallway. There was a small check-out counter in the back, where we drank. The counter was a glass showcase displaying various harmonicas and castanets. No sunlight reached the back of the shop, and it was dim even during the day. In the winter he kept a small space heater by his feet.

There, we'd drink wine, and sometimes we'd empty an entire bottle by ourselves. We talked about music. I learned about the Beatles and he probably learned a few things about Bach.

Late at night, we drank even more. We'd go to a small place run by two middle-aged women that served homely-tasting stews, or a Spanish restaurant in the basement of a building, or a sausage place with a sign out front that claimed to be "The Best in Tokyo."

We often drank until dawn. We would kiss on the street and stagger home.

I wished we were somewhere where we had no attachments or connections.

I wished we were in a city we didn't know at all, and that somewhere in that city was a place we could go home to together.

The Professor used to call us the worst drunks of all time. Shameless, ignorant, hapless drunks.

I open the window to see what kind of night surrounds this place. There's the stream, the village shop, telegraph poles. One of the poles has a sign indicating a school zone. Soko's school.

Soko is sleeping in cream-coloured flannel pyjamas, with a teddy bear sticker on the nail of her big toe. Sitting on the windowsill, I look down at my toes. There's a teddy bear on the nail of my big toe. Soko stuck it there earlier.

"See, we match," Soko said, happily.

I empty the wine in my cup and close the window. The wind is cold enough to sting my skin. Maybe tomorrow we'll have our first snow of the season.

SUNDAY

Cucumbers, *udo* greens, and a fruit of my choice. It's sunny, the wind is blowing gently, and I've got 1,500 yen in my wallet.

Spring came and I started fourth grade. I have the same class teacher as last year, and I'm still in the gardening club. Everyone chooses a committee to join in fourth grade, and I've joined the P.E committee. I don't have to do much, just two things: get everyone into two lines before P.E. (but everyone does it without me doing anything anyway), and bring equipment from the gym storage room to the gym.

I have trouble making up my mind at the store because there are six cucumbers for 320 yen, or three for 280 yen. Getting six would be a better deal, but Mum and I probably can't eat all six by ourselves. There's a thick, white *udo* that looks good. I also decide to get strawberries.

"You're such a good girl, always helping your family with the grocery shopping," the man at the greengrocer's says as he hands me my change.

Rikako and I exchanged a "friendship pact."
The conditions of the pact are:

1. Be loyal (protect each other's secrets).
2. Talk to each other during every recess, even if it's just a couple of words.
3. Walk home together.
4. Do not smile at school until we see each other (keep a straight face even when we say "good morning" to other people). If one of us is absent, then the other person is not allowed to smile all day.
5. Exchange pencils during maths.

We've been good about following the rules for the two weeks since the new school year began.

Mum has a new piano student, a twenty-six-year-old housewife. She just moved here from Tokyo and says she's already "weary" of Takahagi. She comes on Saturday afternoons and I overheard her and Mum talking over tea after her lesson.

"What does 'weary' mean?" I asked Mum when we were taking a bath.

"Weary?" Mum said, as she washed her body with a thin washcloth. She has a nice pale complexion and her body – her round breasts and the smooth curve from her stomach down to her hips – is beautiful.

"Yeah. That new person said today that she was 'weary of this town.'"

"Oh, right," Mum replied, and rinsed the soap off her body. "She's bored. It's when you're sick and tired of something."

"I thought so," I said, as I scooped water from the tub with my cupped hand and let it fall back into the tub, over and over again. "I thought it meant something like that."

Mum laughed. The bathroom smelled of Mum's soap, sweet and rosy. We soaked in the tub together, then I got out after I counted to fifty, drank a glass of milk, and went to bed.

It's become routine for me to drink milk after a bath. Mum doesn't like milk but tells me to drink it every day. She says it's good for me and that she's sure I like it. Apparently this is because Dad likes milk. It's complete nonsense. But strangely enough, I do happen to like it. It's especially delicious right after a bath. It's like my stomach, lungs, heart, and entire body just soak it up.

When I get back from the grocer, I run into our landlady at the entrance of our building.

"Hello," I say.

Seeing that I'm carrying a plastic shopping bag with *udo* greens sticking out, she says, "You've been grocery shopping, Soko? You're such a good girl."

I don't know what to say to her. Both Mum and I know that grocery shopping isn't such a big deal.

The garden is filled with blooming forsythias.

I don't like the spring. It sort of depresses me. And the fact that plants just go ahead and burst with life makes me feel so low.

The cat that seems to belong to Ueda Auto Parts always stares at me when I walk by. Even if it's asleep, it'll open its eyes and glower. Ueda Auto Parts is in an old wooden building painted all white, and its front glass entrance is always wide open. There's a car park next to it where the cat hangs out.

"What is it? What do you want?" I say to the cat, and walk away after I've glared back. It's Sunday and the weather is beautiful. I've checked out three books from the library today, a twenty-minute bus ride away. They're all mystery novels. I'd never stepped foot in a library until I began my journey, but I've since realized what a great system it is. First of all, it helps keep the number of things you own to a minimum. This is important. I've never liked having too much, and this preference for keeping possessions to a bare minimum escalated from around the time I graduated from college. It's so much easier to get rid of things than to keep them.

"In other words, you don't want to take responsibility for your life?" the Professor would sometimes chide me. "Does it mean that you want to float through life forever?"

It's true. Possessions, one by one, tie people down.

The library here is located in a corner of a long concrete building, and it's small but has a good feel to it. I don't drive, but there's a sprawling car park for people that do. The good thing about libraries is that you can order new books, which arrive after a while. And even if you pick out a boring book from the library, it's not as annoying as finding that a book you've bought is a complete letdown.

The doorbell rings as Soko and I are eating breakfast. When I open the door, there's a stocky man I don't recognize standing in the hallway. I stand there at a loss when Soko calls out from behind me, "Mr Takada!"

"Mr Takada?"

I'm still confused, but Mr Takada looks relieved to see Soko.

He turns back towards me and says, "Um, I made this and wondered if you'd like some."

Stewed sweet kidney beans. There's plastic wrap over the small bowl, clouded with steam. The bowl is still warm when he hands it to me.

According to Soko, the man lives upstairs by himself. He must be extremely industrious to be making stewed beans first thing in the morning – that or he has too much time on his hands. I thank him and close the door.

While I don't like the spring, the breeze isn't so bad. I take the long way and walk on the gravel path along the train tracks. The great thing about walks is that they immediately grant you solitude.

When I get home, Soko is at the kitchen table drawing. She says it's a picture of Disneyland. I've promised to take her there during the long weekend in May.

"It's quite a masterpiece," I say, as I open the refrigerator to check on the groceries I asked Soko to pick up. On construction paper, Soko has drawn what appear to be Snow White's dwarves with different coloured crayons.

In the afternoon, I do my homework as I listen to Mum play the piano. I have to work on my math workbook and colour in a blank map. Mum's been playing only pop songs today.

Sometimes I think about Makoto in Imaichi. Makoto's family owns the bathhouse where Mum and I were living, and he's a year older than me. He had a little brother, but he had just been born and wasn't much fun to play with yet. Makoto had Power Rangers figures, a pink ball, and toy trains, and he always let me play with them.

I also think about the old lady in Soka, the one who made me the tote bag when I started elementary school. She lived with her daughter and son-in-law, but apparently wasn't on good terms with her daughter. "Being on good terms" is an expression I learned in Soka. The old lady had tears in her eyes when Mum and I went to say good-bye.

After that, we lived in Kawagoe. Our next-door neighbour there always did laundry in the middle of the night. Except for the scary noise and trembling of the washing machine in the hallway, I have no bad memories of Kawagoe. There were lots of old-fashioned sweet shops near our house and rabbits at my school.

My least favorite place was Takasaki, where we lived for two years before we moved to Imaichi. I don't remember much about the place because I was little, but I hated going to nursery school and cried and cried every time Mum left me there. I would often wake up during naptime and be nervous and scared that I'd get in trouble for being awake. It was dark inside the room but ridiculously bright outside. I'd force myself to lie still, listening to the steady breathing of the other kids.

"Hey, that's 'Close To You.'"

I like the song because it's cheerful and pretty. I can only sing the part that goes, "Just like me, they long to be, close to you," so when Mum gets to that part, I stop doing my homework, run over to the piano, and sing along. When I finish singing, Mum applauds.

I don't remember anything before Takasaki. We supposedly lived a year in Maebashi and a year in a place called Amatsu Kominato.

"We're birds of passage," Mum often says, laughing.

"That sounds exciting." Rikako's eyes light up when I tell her about Mum calling us birds of passage. But I have no idea if being a bird of passage is more exciting than not being a bird of passage, because I've always been one and not the other.

Either way, I think, as I chew on the end of my coloured pencil (a juicy woody flavour oozes out when you bite into the top of a coloured pencil, and it's really good, but Mum yells at me when she catches me doing it)… either way, Mum and I can't *not* be birds of passage. Not until we meet Dad.

It's late afternoon by the time I've played the piano for a couple of hours, so Soko and I head to the ocean. We make it a point to walk out there on days when I don't work in the afternoon. Soko has just finished her homework and says she's bringing along her pink bear.

It's been blissfully sunny all day, but the surf is high and lifts my spirits. I like the ocean better when it's rough than when it's calm. The wind is chilly. It's lovely by the rocks, where we're sprayed with water as the huge waves crash into them. The white beach stretches straight along Route 6, and we walk along the water's edge. Soko soon finds a long, super-thin stick and drags it behind her as she walks. In the other hand, she holds tightly to her pink bear.

"Do you want to walk all the way to the other end?" I point and ask.

Soko thinks about it a bit and says, "Isn't that far?"

"It's not that far." I laugh, and walk ahead. My skirt catches the ocean breeze. "I love walking," I say.

Behind me, Soko sulkily says, "I know."

"Maybe that's why I like long, flared skirts. Because they're easy to walk in."

Soko doesn't say anything so I turn around, seeking a response. Looking a bit perplexed, she says, "Isn't it easier to walk in trousers?"

"I suppose." I don't really like pants. Neither did the Professor. "But the thing about skirts, you know, is that you have to manoeuvre yourself around them, so it feels like you're *really* engaged in the act of walking, don't you think?" I offer, because I have nothing better to say.

"I just don't understand why women all want to dress like men," the Professor used to say all the time. I liked his old-fashioned outlook. I also liked that he wore a hat whenever he went out.

"Look. Glass," I say, picking up a piece of blue glass by my feet and holding it out to Soko. I find pieces of glass on the beach all the time. The corners have been polished off by the waves and the sand. The pieces are smooth and round, with a white and powdery-looking surface. The glass turns translucent when wet, grainy and white when it's dry.

"Doesn't it look like a sweet?"

Once, after saying so, I put a piece in my mouth, which had made Soko laugh. Ever since, we've been collecting sea glass.

I hold on to the glass pieces for Soko because she has both her hands full with the stick and the bear.

"Wait, over here too," Soko says, bringing me one piece after another. I shake my hand with fingers loosely wrapped around the small pieces of glass. They make flat, cold clinking sounds against each other.

The ocean in spring. The clouds remain white as the sky turns increasingly blue-grey.

We'll buy some chicken on the way home, I think to myself. For some reason Soko's bought a ton of cucumbers, so I'm thinking I'll toss them with some cold steamed chicken.

✦ ✦ ✦

On our way home from the beach, we run into the lady from the ramen noodle shop.

"Hello," I say.

The lady, smiling, says, "Long time no see, Soko. Taking a walk?"

Mum smiles and bows, but later asks, "Who was that?"

Mum really doesn't remember people's faces. When I tell her it's the lady from the noodle shop, she says, "If she were wearing her usual white uniform, I'd recognize her." Mum's not very social.

Mum made me wear a navy windbreaker on our way out, but she only has on a cardigan over her blouse. She looks cold and rubs her arms as she walks.

At night, Mum tells me stories about Dad; it's been a while since the last time she did. She doesn't talk about him often, but I love hearing her stories about him.

She tells me two stories today, the one about the Sicilian Kiss at the cottage resort (Mum's favourite), and the one about the airport at dawn.

Mum and Dad once decided to leave everything behind, packed their suitcases, and went to the airport. It was the middle of the night and the roads were empty ("He's such a marvellous driver.") At the airport, they stayed in the car until daybreak. It was a small white car.

At the break of dawn, Dad let Mum off with their things and went to park the car. "The light blue air was cool and the stars were still shining," Mum says. She stood there all alone, waiting. In the cold, clear break of dawn.

When she saw Dad approach, Mum was beside herself with happiness. Even though she'd known that he'd come back. "Watching him walk is an absolute joy," Mum says, that he's "intoxicating to watch." No matter when, and no matter how many times you've seen him.

It didn't matter where they went, as long as it was a foreign country. The further, the better.

They signed up for standby seating (it wasn't high travel season and it was so early in the day that they had no problem getting two tickets), and then they had coffee as they leaned against the counter at a coffee shop.

"And then?" I ask, because Mum's stopped talking. "Where did you two go then?"

Mum smiles and says, "This is where this story ends."

"Why?"

"It just does."

I'm not satisfied with her answer, but I know there's no use asking any further.

"What was Dad like?" I ask instead. It's a question I've asked many times before, but I ask again.

"Oh, well," Mum says, and thinks about it for a while. Then, "Come here," she says, and sits me on her lap. "He has a beautiful spine like yours." She touches my spine. "And he has a forehead that exudes intelligence, like yours," she says as she gently brushes my bangs away from my face. "And he's someone who thinks about things in the most straightforward manner."

"Straightforward?"

"Yes, straightforward," Mum answers. She pronounces it slowly and lovingly, as if it's a special word.

Then we get into bed and the five of us, including Dad, spot-switch. So there's me, Allie, the pink bear, Mum, and Dad, who we pretend is here with us.

We count Dad in the game by leaving a space for him. Allie and the bear are small, but fitting five bodies into two futons isn't easy and is a lot of fun.

"You probably didn't know this," Mum says as we switch spots, "but your dad brought me bliss just by sleeping beside me. Every time, without fail."

According to Mum, Dad's body is very warm, and the hollow below his shoulders is perfectly shaped to fit Mum's cheek.

"Nothing could scare me if I were sleeping beside him," Mum says. But she's scared of everything, so I think that's a bit of a tall tale.

THE PROFESSOR

I'm not blaming anyone for my love affair. It had nothing to do with anyone or anything except the two of us. When we met and fell in love, I wasn't unhappy with my life. At least not to the extent my mother, aunt, and cousins say I was.

I climb the long stone stairway leading to the shrine.

The shrine is one of my favourite places here. It's quiet and there's never anyone around, but it's always swept clean – pure and spotless. I came here often on my walks in the summer because the lush green and the cool air felt good. *Shinto* rope festoons hang across the traditional gate of the *torii* at the top and bottom of the stone steps. The *torii* at the bottom is grey, the colour of stone, but the one up above is damp and covered in moss the colour of green tea.

I stand between the shrine's two stone guard dogs and press my palms together in front of my chest. I don't leave any money in the offering box.

Though I'm not the religious type, I find it sort of calming to be here like this. Far away, a crow caws once.

Not once have I regretted anything. Not my marriage to the Professor, and not my love affair.

I've never regretted anything, but every once in a while I'm suddenly overcome with terror, because I've come so far away.

I like the view from the top of the stone steps. Nothing blocks the view all the way to the mountains far off in the distance, the sky, trees, paved roads, and roofs that dot the landscape.

Skipping down the steps two at a time, I maintain a steady rhythm – tap, tap tap, tap, tap – as I go. What am I doing next? What should I do? What in the world will happen?

It's not long before the paved road ends. The rest of the way is dirt or gravel. I take the back roads home.

Soko doesn't resemble me when I was a child. She actually looks more like my cousin Mihoko. Soko's a good student and looks older than she actually is.

"Don't give your mum too much heartache," Mihoko used to say to me. She's two years older, and her sister, Kaho, is two years younger than me. I got along better with Kaho.

"Yoko, you're weird," Kaho would often say.

I'd done badly in school since I was a child. I was good at the piano but had no other talents. I was always causing so much trouble for my parents. I was hospitalised for pneumonia, ran away from home, and hurt a friend of mine in a fight.

I went to the same private middle school as my cousins but left halfway through. The records say it was my decision to transfer to a state school nearby, but of course, I'd been kicked out.

At the time, I had ridiculous hair. It was bright pink. The hair stylist who dyed it called it "cotton candy pink," and Kaho called it "the colour of dolls on *iroha* blocks." I had no idea what she was talking about.

As I walk, I gaze at the stretches of gravel – more like driveways than gardens – between the houses and their front gates. In front of each house, flowers bloom in a multitude of colours in the autumn air. There's one house with a big aubergine growing in a pot by the front door.

Over a year has passed since we moved here. It's about time I started thinking about our next move.

For the first time in a while, I walk all the way home from school on my heels for fun. My calves ache a little, but it's no big deal. And to think it used to be so hard for me when I was younger.

When I get home, Mum's frying doughnuts for me.

"Where's Maho?"

"She went home."

The kitchen is filled with the sweet smell of doughnuts. Some of my pictures are taped to the glass door of the cupboard.

"Oh. That was short." Last night, Maho spent the night at our house. She'd had a fight with her live-in boyfriend. It wasn't the first time. Sometimes, like last night, she stays over for just one night, and other times she'll stay for about three.

Maho is Mum's friend who also works at Daisy. She has long hair and is really pretty. She knows a lot about Pokemon and sings Speed songs with me when we go to karaoke.

"Off you go and wash your hands," Mum says.

Last week, there was a sports day at my school.

I was in the group gymnastics performance and the obstacle course race. It was a nice day out. Mum packed our lunches in the morning in high spirits, and came to watch. She also participated in the parents' tug-of-war. Mum and Rikako's dad were on the same team, and the two of us cheered for them like crazy. We were so wrapped up in the match that we didn't realize that we were standing bowlegged with our feet digging into the ground, as if we were the ones pulling the rope. It cracked us up.

"I like the music they play at school sports days," Mum said. She was drinking tea from her thermos, her face sweaty after playing tug-of-war.

"I like all the colourful paper decorations, too."

Mum likes weird stuff.

When I came in third out of eight in the obstacle course, Mum became overly excited and crushed me in her arms. She squeezed my head again and again and with a look of utter delight said, "You've got your dad's genes."

I didn't think placing third out of eight people was that big a deal, which I told her. Mum looked surprised. Then, in all seriousness, she said, "Well, what do you expect? You're my daughter, too."

My favourite part of sports days is lunch. The fresh air mixed with the smell of seaweed from everyone's rice balls makes it feel like such a special occasion.

At lunch, we also ate the boiled chestnuts the landlady had brought over for us that morning.

✦ ✦ ✦

A bittersweet smile sweeps across my face whenever I see the way Soko leaves her sneakers by the front door. She's becoming more and more like her father. Even the way her left shoe lies slightly in front of her right is just like her father's shoes after he's kicked them off.

After I finish frying the doughnuts, I pour Soko a glass of milk and make myself some coffee. An old song comes on the radio and I hum along. It's 'Heartache Tonight' by the Eagles.

"So, you like to dance?" the Professor once said, smiling. I was listening to music in my room. "Your shoulders move so freely."

I can't help but move my body when I listen to music I really like.

"I like watching you dance."

The Professor was a kind man. He was skinny and tall, and wore small, round-rimmed glasses. He had a full head of soft hair that was combed back.

"It's not that I'm against it," my mother had said almost pleadingly, when I told her that I wanted to marry the Professor. "But what's the rush?"

When I met the Professor, I no longer had pink hair. By then, I had become a quiet college student with few friends.

The Professor was the head of the piano department. I took private lessons with him for four years.

We got married as soon as I graduated.

"He hadn't broken it off yet with the other girl," Maho said last night. It was after Soko had fallen asleep, and Maho and I were drinking Wild Turkey and water on the rocks.

"I kicked him real hard a dozen times. He covered his head with a pillow, but I bet his body's all bruised."

She was angry, but she didn't look like she'd completely lost it.

"I don't know, he might have a broken rib or two," she said. She sounded a little worried.

"Do you have any intention of breaking up with him?" I knew the answer but thought I'd ask anyway. Maho smiled weakly and touched the ice in her bourbon with her finger.

"Mrs Inoue from Class 3 is going on maternity leave. She said good-bye to us today during the morning assembly," Soko says as she eats a doughnut. "She wears her hair in braids and is so cute. I'm going to miss her."

"She's cute?" I ask, as I sip my coffee and light a cigarette.

"Yeah," Soko says, with a know-it-all look on her face. "She's always wearing cute maternity clothes, too."

"Hmm."

The coffee is a bit too strong. A harsh bitterness spreads inside my mouth. "What about your class teacher? Isn't she cute?" I ask.

Soko shrugs and says with a resigned look, "Yeah, she's cute."

I remember a lot of things about the Professor. To the very end, he and I never had any physical contact beyond holding hands, but I loved the temperature and dryness of those bony hands. His wedding band suited his hand well. It was a simple silver ring, and he never took it off.

I had no complaints about the Professor aside from one thing – the fact that he expected nothing from me.

"It's not about you," he said, looking at me ruefully. "I'm the kind of person who can't expect anything from anyone."

I felt forsaken. "That's the same thing as not expecting anything from me." But it wasn't. It was worse.

It might have had to do with the fact that he'd been abandoned by his father as a child, or that he had experienced two failed marriages before he met me. But I didn't know for certain.

There's only one thing I know for certain. That I, too, eventually left the Professor.

"So you're leaving me, too," he said. "Even though he's no longer here." It was late at night. Ordinarily, the Professor would have been fast asleep.

"I'm sorry," I said, as I stared at the Professor's slippers. His black, soft, goat-skin slippers. They were the only slippers he wore. Whenever they became worn out, he'd go to the Mitsukoshi department store to buy a new pair of the exact same ones.

"But don't think that I'm immoral," I said, looking straight at the Professor.

"Immoral?" The eyes behind his glasses took on a slightly amused, quizzical look.

"Mm. He called me immoral, but I'm not. Just because he's gone, I can't go on living with you like this." As I spoke, I was thinking about how the Professor's mother would be worried. It was already very late.

The Professor's mother was in her eighties and lived by herself. Every night, the Professor went to her house three minutes away to spend the night.

"He told you that you were immoral?" The Professor looked confused. Confused and uncomprehending.

Actually, what he'd said was that *we* were immoral. "We really are immoral. In a destructive way. Didn't you know, Silly? That love is a special privilege of the immoral?"

"He doesn't understand you," the Professor said, with an ironic smile.

"Do you want another glass of milk?" I ask, and Soko shakes her head.

"No."

After we finish the doughnuts, we clean up our plates and read. The past two or three days, Soko has been engrossed in a book called *Caravan*.

◆　◆　◆

At night, after Mum leaves for work, I play the piano. 'Pastorale' is one of the few songs I can play all the way to the end. I can only play part of 'Valiant Knight', so I play the same part over and over again.

I feel restless.

At dinner, Mum hinted at moving again. "What kind of place do you want to live in next?" she asked

"Are we moving?" I replied, and even though Mum said that she didn't know yet, I knew. I could tell from experience. "It's only been a year," I protested.

But Mum just said with a vacant look, "It has, hasn't it?"

I don't know why, but as I play the piano, my eyes fill with tears. I remember my friendship pact with Rikako and feel like I'm betraying her. I squeeze my eyes shut. The tears don't fall; they only moisten my lower eyelids and lashes. I pound on the piano. 'Valiant Knight' is a heroic song, so it's just right for banging. Even if it's only part of the song.

I imagine myself announcing to my class that I'll be changing schools. I'll stand on the podium at the front of the classroom and say, "Thanks for everything. It was fun, even though I was only here for a short time," and bow. I imagine my going away party. The one that my classmates will throw for me during fifth period on a Wednesday. I imagine the fancy card everyone will sign along with a few parting words, the candy that will be laid out on floral-print paper napkins. Then I'll clean out my locker. It won't be the end of the school year yet, so I'll be the only one taking everything out of her locker. Mum will probably pick me up since I'll have a lot of stuff to take home, like my shoes and gym clothes and calligraphy stuff. The two of us will walk through the playground and leave the school grounds. For an unknown place. The way we always do.

After I turn off the radio and get under the covers, I think about Dad, about the day I finally meet him.

According to Mum, Dad's face is "so very beautiful" when he smiles.

"What does someone look like when they're 'so very beautiful?'" I asked, and Mum replied with great confidence, "Like your dad, when he smiles."

"You know what I mean," I'd huffed. Mum laughed, said she was sorry, and explained to me what his smiling face was like.

"It's the face of someone with a beautiful heart. It's absolutely radiant. Anyone who saw your dad's smile would know right away that he has a beautiful heart."

Mum gets such a tender look on her face when she talks about Dad. She speaks more slowly than usual and chooses her words carefully. Kind of like the way she picks pieces of sea glass off the beach.

I've imagined myself meeting Dad so many times. Whenever and wherever it happens, I smile when I see him. Then I say, "Nice to meet you."

And Dad will probably say, "Nice to meet you, too." We might shake hands. Dad will notice that I have his spine and forehead.

"How's it going?" That's probably what he'll say next. With a smile that's "so very beautiful."

Thinking about Dad makes me feel a bit better.

✦ ✦ ✦

Early in November, I decide where we're moving next: Sakura, Chiba. I haven't told Soko yet, but she seems to have a sneaking suspicion that we're leaving Takahagi.

It doesn't matter where we go. Takahagi turned out to be a lot more comfortable than I expected, which is why I decided to move earlier than I'd planned. I'm scared that I'll find myself getting used to life here. I feel like he'll never find me if I settle down somewhere, no matter where it is.

"I'll be back," he said that hot afternoon in September. Wherever you are, whatever you're doing, I swear I will find you again, Yoko."

"No matter where I am?" I'd laughed at the time. "I won't go anywhere. I'll be waiting here until you come back. I won't move a step."

I can't risk fitting into a place where he isn't. Because I'm not meant to be anywhere he's not.

Sakura seems like a peaceful place. It happened to come up in conversation at Daisy, and Maho – who'd seen an ad for new houses for sale in Sakura – said that it was supposed to be a convenient place to live. So I went to have a look and made my decision. There's a big piano school there, and luckily they're looking for instructors.

I figure I'll go again, this time with Soko, to look for a place to live.

"Why did you make such a promise?" My mother demanded nearly ten years ago, looking as if she was about to burst into tears. "You don't really intend to keep such a promise, do you?"

Of course I did. Especially since it was a promise I had made to the Professor.

"I want you to leave Tokyo," the Professor had said with a truly pained look on his face. That was the only condition of our divorce.

"I can't bear to think it might be you every time I see a young woman with short hair." His voice trembled. "And I can't bear to think it might be Soko every time I see a little girl."

By then I no longer saw the Professor as my husband or as the piano professor who'd won numerous awards and chaired the piano department at a university. He just looked like a lonely, elderly man.

On my way out, the Professor took all the ATM cards out of his wallet and gave them to me. There were three.

"Take these. The pin number for each one of them is your birthday."

I never used them. I can only hope that I didn't hurt the Professor's feelings even more by not using them.

I stick my hand out of the covers, fishing for my cigarettes and lighter. I can tell Soko's in the kitchen having breakfast.

I rub my cold face with one hand, put a cigarette in my mouth, and light it.

I listen carefully to every single sound Soko makes. The sound of her carrying her dishes to the sink, the sound of her opening her backpack and checking that she has all her things, the sound of her brushing her teeth at the sink.

Soko will soon come to say good-bye. She'll timidly crack open the sliding door. When she does, I'll invite her to visit Sakura on Sunday to look for our new home. She won't be surprised. She'll stiffen for a moment but will no doubt say, "okay."

I put out my cigarette in the ashtray and lie face-up again The stains in the wooden grains of the ceiling look like they form some kind of a design. I try singing a Rod Stewart song, but I'm hoarse and my voice cracks.

When I need you, I just close my eyes and I'm with you
And all that I so want to give you it's only a…

I wonder where he is. Where is he and what is he doing now?

SAKURA, 1999

The Doobie Brothers' "Long Train Runnin" was blaring from the speakers. A feverish energy filled the dance floor, the air thick with the sickly sweet perfume of college girls in flashy outfits, combing their long hair back with their fingers as they swayed their hips. It was a sweet, animal-like smell. Back then, any disco that made even the slightest effort was packed, night after night. No matter how crowded the floor, though, I was always surrounded by a small pocket of empty space. Maybe people were afraid they'd be sprayed with sweat if they came too close. I danced furiously.

I was seventeen. I danced in tank tops and miniskirts, but was soaked in sweat in no time. Even in the dead of winter.

Sometimes guys would approach me, emboldened by alcohol. I'd invite them to dance with me but they'd mostly just stand there, pestering me with questions about my age and pressing me to sit down for a drink. I'd keep dancing though, and eventually they'd give up – or were turned off, maybe – and go back to their friends.

Dancing felt great. For me, it was merely a fun and refreshing activity. I danced until I was exhausted.

"So it was like going to the gym," he'd said with a smile when I reminisced about those days. His powerful smile – on that face with the most beautiful bone structure – could always bring happiness to every cell in my body.

It was true. For me, discos were like sports clubs. Once my body was satiated, I would knock back a cold drink at the bar on the way to the lockers, wipe the sweat off my face, throw on my coat, and take off.

I'd leave and find myself in the cold, huge, lonely Tokyo landscape that I neither loved nor hated.

I was born in the middle of winter in 1962, and grew up in the very centre of Tokyo. To me, Tokyo was like a school playground – boring and dusty, tiny yet vast.

I was a horrible daughter, even though my father lovingly called me by my nickname, Yo, and often let me sit on his lap, and my mother, a full-time housewife, hand-sewed dresses and things for me.

Since I've been on my journey with Soko, I've often thought about my parents.

"What are you going to be when you grow up, Yo?" my father once asked me.

"Topo Gigio," I answered.

"Really? Topo Gigio?" my father laughed gleefully.

"Yo says she's going to be Topo Gigio when she grows up," my father told my mother.

She laughed, too, cheerfully. "You're a funny girl, Yoko," she said.

My mother was always wearing tight, knee-length skirts with form-fitting tops and jumpers. When she went out she wore a perfume called Mitsouko.

I have been given three treasures in my life. The first I received when I was six. It was a piano. Black, shiny, and beautiful—and when I opened the lid, there was the distinct smell of wood and varnish.

For the sake of my parents, I want to make it clear that I hold myself responsible for all the things I've done, like getting a friend hurt when I was in elementary school, dyeing my hair "cotton candy" and dropping out of school, running away from home time and again, and being cited for juvenile delinquency by the police. I was the cause and result of it all. My parents were never to blame. I loved my parents.

It was simply that I didn't know what to do with myself. I had absolutely no clue.

"It's because you literally have no sense of direction, Yoko," my true love once said with a gentle look in his eyes. "You were really far gone, weren't you?"

I wanted to cry. I was suddenly overcome with emotion and I didn't know what to do. I'd always been alone. I hadn't become Topo Gigio. I'd never thought I was down on my luck, but I'd been bored. I hadn't understood what I was living for. I hadn't understood what I was supposed to do or why I had to go on living. That is, until I met him.

✦ ✦ ✦

The day of our move, the three of us – Maho, Mum, and I – go to a family restaurant for breakfast. The weather's really nice and the soapwort by the bus stop is in full bloom.

I order the breakfast combo with pancakes, sausage, and scrambled eggs. The pancakes are flimsy and get soggy when I pour syrup on them.

We all eat a lot and don't talk much because we don't know what to talk about. The restaurant is bright and smells like bacon.

After we finish eating, Mum and Maho keep getting coffee refills and continue to smoke. The bracelet on Maho's left wrist catches the sun and glitters as she moves her arm.

Maho pays the bill. It's a going-away breakfast.

Once we're outside, Mum draws back her shoulders like a peacock, turns her face up just slightly, and closes her eyes.

"Such a pleasant day," she says with a smile. Mum cries easily, but she never cries or looks upset when we move.

"Let's get together again, soon," Maho and I promise each other. When we meet up, we'll wear matching nail stickers and go to karaoke to sing Speed's latest songs.

"I hope you find your boyfriend, Yoko," Maho says.

"Thanks," Mum smiles. And with a look of utmost confidence, she says, "It'll be fine," as if Maho is the one waiting and Mum is trying to comfort her.

Sakura is an interesting place, cheerful and laid back. There are sculptures all around town. There's also an old shopping arcade, and it's quiet here. A plastic statue of a boy who looks like he's from outer space stands in front of the electrical shop. Whenever we walk by the battered statue, Mum pats it. He has antennas sticking out of both his ears and rubber boots on his feet, and gives a thumbs-up with his gloved right hand.

Mum teaches at a piano school two train stations away, but also works three nights a week at a bar. Having two jobs keeps her emotionally balanced, and plus, this way she can put more bread on the table. "Putting bread on the table" means earning a living, so it doesn't mean she actually brings home more bread. It just means we have more money to spend.

Sakura isn't by the ocean like Takahagi, so on weekends we walk to Joshi Park instead of the beach. The park is huge. It has trees and grass, there's lots of sky, and the air's nice and fresh.

We went to the park the day before yesterday, too.

Mum was a bit tired that day. I can easily tell when she's tired because she gets dark shadows around her eyes and her voice loses all its energy.

"Maybe you're smoking too much," I suggested, and Mum feigned surprise.

"No way!" she replied. "You're joking, right? You know I get my nutrients from cigarettes." She immediately took out her cigarettes from a small handbag, put one in her mouth, and lit up.

"You're like a little child," I said, pretending to be annoyed.

"Mind your own business," Mum said, and blew smoke out of her mouth.

We sat on the bank of the dry moat at the park and drank coffee with lots of milk that Mum had made and brought in a small thermos. We don't drink coffee from vending machines. Mum says there's a "murderous" amount of sugar in that kind of coffee.

"How's your new school?" Mum asked. It'd been a month since I started school here.

"So-so," I said.

"Really," was all Mum said.

Rikako and I are pen pals now. She promised that she would write and asked me to write her, too. We added a few things to our friendship pact:

6. Write to each other about any changes, incidents, and discoveries right away.
7. Meet again.
8. Never forget each other.

Since we moved, Mum's been gone a lot of the time when I get home from school. I could go see her at the community centre where she teaches piano (she tells me I'm allowed to visit whenever I want to) but I haven't been there yet.

✦ ✦ ✦

Our building is old, but I like that our flat is in the corner of the first floor and we have a garden. It's a small garden full of weeds.

The new bar where I work is called Tsumiki. It's a pretty small place, with bar seating only. I work there three times a week, from eight to one. The owner is a man, an old friend of the manager at Daisy.

"I hear you're from Tokyo," a customer said to me last night. "I am, too. Kanda. But we bought a house here last year. It's still a reasonable commute to Tokyo from here. But when it comes down to it, it's pretty dull and provincial out here compared to Kanda."

The sun shines beautifully here. It's a town that feels uncomplicated.

"It's a nice place, isn't it?" That's what he would say.

Here, too, I've stopped by the music shop. I went without any great expectations, but when I walked inside I was so nervous I thought I was going to fall apart. And even though I already knew it, I was almost more relieved than disappointed when the person stringing a guitar inside the shop turned out not to be my true love.

The day before yesterday, Soko and I went to Joshi Park. When I asked Soko how school was, she said it was "so-so." So-so. I can only take her word for it.

Summer's almost here. The grass on the bank was a dewy green, and its sweet fragrance floated in the air.

"There's this strange boy," Soko said, as she pulled a handful of grass out of the ground.

"A strange boy?"

"Yeah, in my class."

"What's this boy like?" I asked.

"He's really fat."

"That's it?"

"No. He doesn't talk, either. He just doesn't fit in."

"More than you, the new girl?"

Soko fell silent, as if I'd hurt her feelings. She then nodded reluctantly and said, "I get along better than him with everyone."

"Hmm."

I thought about Soko's life, which I'm clueless about. This life of hers in which she is repeatedly forced to start over without any regard for her own wishes.

"You're a tough girl."

"Not really," Soko answered sullenly, and unscrewed the top of the thermos. "Maybe I have a certain knack for getting along anywhere."

I was suddenly reminded of my own childhood.

"You have absolutely no knack for getting by in the world," my mother had often said to me. I had no idea what having a "knack" entailed.

My mother.

My mother blames the Professor. "That man has no right to drive you and Soko out of this city," she'd raged, with a terrifying look on her face.

She was wrong, though. We weren't forced to leave. I chose my own path. I chose to live with the Professor, and I chose to leave him and the city.

Then, it was just Soko and me, the two of us.

I have nothing to ask of Soko, the third gift I've been given. She's healthy and bright, and there's nothing more I can ask for. What I want is for her to savour life, to pay attention, with both mind and body. Always. The way he does.

The area around Chiku Centre train station is kind of like an amusement park. There's nothing beyond the immediate vicinity, but it's teeming with life right around the station. Especially around dusk – the lights from the doughnut shop, the thirty-one-storey block of flats, and Saty, the giant supermarket. The piano school where I work is on the outskirts of this pseudo amusement park complex.

I have more adult students than children. Some are schoolchildren who come on their way home from school. It has a more open, casual feel to it than the Suzuki school did.

The instructors are allowed to play the piano between lessons. I play some jazz today – like 'These Foolish Things' and 'Body and Soul' – for the first time in a while. The girl who works at the reception desk brings me some coffee.

"That's lovely. Can you play 'Stars Fell on Alabama?'"

So I play that, too. The part-time receptionist apparently takes jazz drum lessons, and knows quite a bit of jazz herself.

"How about 'My One and Only Love?'"

"Sorry," I tell her, "I've forgotten how it goes. I haven't played it in such a long time."

It isn't a complete lie. I really haven't played it in a long time. But I haven't forgotten it. There's no way I ever could. A song he'd sung to me with a voice so gentle that it almost seemed odd, such a contrast to his strong body.

"Is your speciality jazz?" Her question manages to just keep me grounded in reality.

"No, classical. You might find it hard to believe, but Bach is my thing."

When I get home, Soko is drawing. It's a picture of an elephant, a butterfly, and a monkey.

"I'm home," I say, crouching down behind her.

"Hi." Soko turns her head in my direction, but she looks like she's a million miles away. Out of habit, though, she slips both arms around my neck.

"Are you hungry?" I ask, as I wash my hands and stand at the kitchen counter.

After a while, Soko shouts, "I want to draw a scarf for the elephant!" And then, "What colour do you think it should be?"

"Navy blue!" With a kitchen knife in my hand, I slightly raise my voice, too. It's hard to hear each other because Soko is sitting with her legs in front of her on the *tatami* mat in the Japanese-style room with her drawing board, instead of at the kitchen table. Plus, there's a game – football or hockey or baseball or something like that – on the radio that's hanging from a hook on the fridge.

"Navy?" Soko doesn't seem to agree.

"What color do you think it should be?" I broil some salmon and steam a few vegetables, which I season lightly with some consommé powder.

"I guess light blue and white polka dots."

"Put your stuff away and go wash your hands. Dinner's almost ready."

After dinner, Soko and I go to the public bath. There's a bath in our flat but it's tiny, and since there's a nice public bath nearby, we go there a lot on nights when I don't work at Tsumiki. I love big baths. It's also pretty interesting to watch all the women with different body types walking about in the nude.

"I wonder how Makoto and his mum are doing," Soko says in the tub. "I wonder how big his little brother is now."

I'm always surprised by what a great memory Soko has, unlike me. Makoto is one of the boys from the family whose house we boarded in. I don't even remember his face anymore.

"Do you want to see him?" I ask. Soko thinks about it a bit and says, "Not really." That's one of Soko's pet phrases.

"I wonder how the old lady in Soka's doing." Seems like Soko's in a sentimental mood today.

"Do you want to go see her sometime?" I suggest, but she dismisses it with another nonchalant "not really." Her back is so small. There are strands of stray wet hair plastered to her shoulders.

Sometimes I'm surprised how positive Mum is. Takahagi is probably already "in the box" for her. I can't believe it.

After we get out of the bath and weigh ourselves on the scale, I drink milk and Mum has some mineral water.

The walk home feels so good with our wet hair down and our towels hanging on our shoulders. We sing 'Close to You' (I only sing the parts I know) as we walk.

While Mum reads, I sit next to her and write Rikako a letter. It goes like this:

Dear Rikako,

How are you? Today, we had art at school. I think I told you in my last letter that I joined the art committee instead of the P.E. committee. I think this was a good choice because I've always been better at art than P.E.

We also had maths today. Don't worry. I remembered to use the pencil you gave me.

There's a pretty interesting landmark in Sakura. It's a windmill. Isn't that weird? It's a huge, impressive windmill. It's near Inba Marsh. You should come visit me, and we can go cycling around the marsh. The windmill doesn't move most of the time, though. I asked the man sitting at the entrance of the windmill when it does, and he told me, "It depends on the wind." But on Saturdays and Sundays, the windmill moves even when there's no wind. Mum says that they use electricity to move it for the tourists.

How is everything with you? Please write. Take care.

From,

Soko

"What are you reading?" I ask after I finish the letter, seal it carefully, and put a stamp on the envelope. Mum shows me the cover, and I read the title out loud. "*My Wife Dies Twice.*"

"Is it a mystery?"

"Yep," Mum says, her eyes still moving over the words on the page.

"Aren't you going to bed?" I ask, laying down on Mum's lap.

"You go ahead."

"Why don't you read in bed?"

Mum tries to read for another five seconds, but then starts laughing. "You're so tempting." She closes her book, presses her lips against my head, and squeezes me tight. "You're like your dad, the way you interrupt my reading."

She tickles me, and I laugh. "Let's go to sleep holding hands," I say.

"It would be my pleasure," Mum replies. I brush my teeth, lay Allie and the pink bear to my right, get under the covers, and slide my hand into Mum's futon. Mum's fingers are icy.

I close my eyes. "Good night."

"Good night," Mum says. Before long, Mum lets go of my hand for just a moment, abruptly stands up, and turns off the light. Darkness falls on my eyelids, and just the tiny orange nightlight remains on.

Pretending to toss in my sleep, I slide into Mum's futon.

SUMMER

Mum apparently loved rainy mornings when she and Dad were on their really long trip a long time ago. She sometimes tells me nostalgically about waking up in Paris, where the small hotel room swelled with the presence of rain, how quiet it was, and how if she listened carefully, sure enough, she'd hear the rain falling. The bed would be dishevelled, and usually Dad's body would be half uncovered. He had big shoulders and his body was always hot. Mum says he was "just perfect" and couldn't help but kiss him all over.

On rainy mornings, Mum could barely drag herself out of bed. Mum and Dad would hold each other, kiss, whisper sweet nothings, smooth the hair away from each other's foreheads, kiss again and again, hold hands, and just lie there, quietly listening to the rain.

They would finally work up the resolve to get up. The bakery a minute's walk away was filled with "the sweet fragrance of pastries," and Mum and Dad would suddenly remember that "smells are so much more intense on rainy days." With coffee and croissants, they would return to their room, dive back into bed, and have breakfast, glued to each other. In the small hotel room, quiet and full of joy.

But I know. Mum's never been on a trip with Dad. Not once.

It's so exhilarating to work – to feel that one is being useful.

"Yoko, you're so diligent," the manager said to me last night. I seem to like having things to do. Like having glasses to fill, customers' stories to listen to, ashtrays to empty out, glasses and pitchers to wash, curtains to be dry-cleaned, rooms to clean, doormats to be sent out to the exchange and cleaning service. Tasks that I can tackle one by one until they are eventually complete.

I sometimes think that I should've worked when I was married to the Professor.

It's been four months since we arrived in Sakura, and life here has been fulfilling. I teach piano in the mornings on Tuesdays and Thursdays, and all day on Wednesdays, Fridays, and Saturdays, then I'm off on Sundays and Mondays. The lessons are an hour each, and most students come once a week. Some have lessons two or three times a week, and some of the kids that only take only one lesson a week come by all the time just to hang out. It's a mixed bunch.

Mrs Oshita began taking piano lessons when she was seventy (it's never too late to start). She's been making slow but steady progress, and now in her sixth year, is about to finish playing Burgmüller. Sometimes her husband comes to pick her up at the end of her lesson. He's a small, energetic old man with a bald head.

I only have lessons in the morning today, and Soko is out when I get home. I'm so lonely when she's not around. I make sandwiches for the two of us and wait for her to return. She doesn't come home, though, so I eat alone. Then I read until late afternoon.

The floor is a black and white chequered pattern, and the ceiling is white. Just inside the entrance, to the left, are the reception counter and a gift shop. Because of the glass walls, the inside gets a lot of sun. There's even a coffee shop in the back. A bunch of square pieces of art hang in the stairwell. The only gripe I have about the place is that there's no backrest on the black leather bench. But admission is free at this public museum, which is great. It's been a week since school let out for the summer, and I've been coming here every day to get away from the heat.

We don't have an air-conditioner in our new flat. Mum seems fine with it, her excuse being that "air-conditioning isn't good for you, anyway." Apparently the air-conditioners at both the bar and the piano school where she works are on full-blast, to the point that it's too cold.

At the museum I do my homework, read books, and play "Spy,"

a game I recently invented. I pretend that I'm a grown-up spy on a mission, disguised as a kid. I observe my surroundings carefully and quickly report back on my secret transceiver, which is actually just an eraser. I'll say things like "all normal" or "two suspicious individuals on the premises." Though the lady at reception probably thinks of *me* as a suspicious individual.

On the last day of the first trimester, Mum and I went to a sushi-go-round restaurant. Mum was happy because I'd been given good marks in my report.

"I don't care if you get bad grades, but it makes me happy knowing you do so well in school," she'd said. Whatever. She also said, "You probably take after your father."

Mum's favourite sushi is flounder and mine is fatty tuna. Mum's second favourite is conger eel, and mine is the cucumber roll.

"Did Dad get good marks?" I asked, drinking weak tea from a big teacup.

"Of course," Mum answered. Then she thought about it for a moment. "I've never seen his reports," she said, "but I'm sure he got good marks. I mean, he's extremely witty."

It seemed like too much trouble to explain to Mum that being witty and getting good grades aren't necessarily the same thing, so I didn't even try. "Hmm," I said instead, and reached for a plate of egg sushi. "Can I get some fruit jelly, too?"

With a loving grin, Mum said "Of course."

"Nojima-san?" I hear a meek voice. I turn around to find Numata-kun, the really fat boy from my class. Because he wears the kind of trousers that are for grown-ups, he looks like a middle-aged man even though he's a child.

"What are you doing?" he asks, looking really puzzled. He takes in my books and notebooks and bag spread out on the bench as if he'd never seen such a sight before.

"Nothing, really," I say. "What are *you* doing here?"

For a moment, Numata-kun looks taken aback. Then, "Oh, my mum works over there," he says, as he points to the museum coffee shop in the back.

"Oh, really," I say, a bit embarrassed. Numata-kun obviously has more reason to be here than I do. "I was doing my homework," I say reluctantly, and I start putting away my things. "We don't have air-conditioning at home. But it's nice and cool here."

"Why are you putting your stuff away?"

"I'm going home."

"Hmm," Numata-kun says.

"Bye, then," I say, and leave the coolness of the museum.

When I get home, Mum is reading.

"Hi, Mum."

It's a fifteen-minute walk from the museum to our flat. In those fifteen minutes, I've got all sticky with sweat.

"Lunch?" Mum looks up from her book and asks.

"Later. I'm going to take a shower first."

The sliding glass door facing the garden is wide open, and through the screen I can hear the wind chimes Mum bought. They're small, but they make a piercing sound that's startling. Mum says the sound has a "cooling effect" on her, but I don't like it very much.

Why does taking a shower late in the afternoon in the summer suddenly make me so drowsy? After a late lunch, I lie down by Mum's feet where she's reading. Enjoying the sensation of the *tatami* mat on my skin, I doze off. I hear the wind chimes far away at the edge of my consciousness.

Later, Mum and I go for a walk. It's a light blue evening. As soon as the sun goes down, the temperature drops. Mum listens to music on my Walkman as we walk.

The tree-lined street leading to Joshi Park is a favourite of ours. It's a big street with a middle school on the right. It's the school I'll be going to the year after next if we're still here. I'll be wearing a grey gym uniform (the boys are issued green gym uniforms, and the girls get grey).

"It smells nice," I say, looking at the sky in the distance. "What is it?"

Mum lets the hems of her skirt billow in the wind when she walks. I can see her bare ankles and red sandals.

"It's the smell of evening."

It's strange, but all summer evenings smell the same no matter where you are.

✦ ✦ ✦

Business is good at Tsumiki. At Daisy, we had a lot of regulars who stayed for hours on end, but the customers at Tsumiki are mostly working people in suits who come in groups of two or three for a quick drink. There's the occasional customer who gets plastered, but for the most part our customers are well behaved. A lot of them seem to live around Chiku Centre and Yukarigaoka.

"Here you go." Here it's the manager – not the customers – who often brings me chocolate.

"What's the occasion? These are really expensive chocolates."

"Do you like them?"

The manager is a middle-aged man with a golf tan who's always wearing a black polo shirt.

"You really shouldn't spoil your employees like this." I make light of the gift as much as I possibly can, trying to maintain a safe distance. The manager is single.

"I'll leave you to take care of the rest, all right?"

It's part of my routine to have a cup of coffee after I see the manager off at night, just the way I used to with Maho at Daisy. Then I lock up and get on my bike. I head straight home to Soko.

It's a star-filled night. It was only after I left Tokyo that I realized how many stars there are in the night sky.

I hum a Rod Stewart song as I pedal my bike.

I like the summer. Summer was when God gave me my second gift. The sun flooded the city. Every day, we escaped our respective lives to see each other in the dizzying heat. Our meetings felt both like a split second and an eternity.

Summer, though, was also when God took away that gift.

If we'd known about Soko, would things have turned out any differently?

When I get home, Soko is already asleep. I shower and get under the covers right away. Soko's been putting out my futon for me every night for years now.

Soko is sensitive to the heat, and is sleeping with a folded blanket over her belly, with her arms and legs exposed. I listen to her faint, even breaths and notice beads of sweat on her forehead. I fan Soko's legs with a paper fan.

The piano school and Tsumiki are closed next week for the Buddhist holiday, Obon, and Soko and I are planning to go to the beach.

"Let's go to the Boso coast," I'd suggested a few days ago as I looked at a map.

"Fine," Soko muttered.

"You like the ocean, don't you?" I asked, and with a brooding look, Soko nodded yes. She was stringing beads, and the kitchen table was covered in beautiful specks of colour.

"But…" Soko looked at me imploringly as she raised her head. "If we're going to the beach we might as well go to Takahagi, don't you think? You liked the ocean there," she added.

"Hmm."

I had no intention of going to Takahagi. Looking back or developing strong bonds will only tie me down. "Why not Izu? There are hot springs there."

Soko frowned. "Boso is fine."

Soko was making a thin bracelet with a white floral pattern on red ribbon.

I put down the fan and lie down but can't fall asleep. How unusual; I generally have no trouble sleeping. I stare at the white covers glowing orange in the nightlight for a long, long time.

The biggest change since Mum and I moved here is that we've started having breakfast together. It's because Mum goes to work in the mornings now. But what I eat for breakfast is still the same: cereal, eggs, tea, and sometimes fruit. The English-language news and the weather report are on the radio hanging from the refrigerator.

"Seems like it's going to be another hot day," Mum says as she covers half her face with her hand, yawning. "Are you going to the museum?"

I tell her I probably will. Mum's teaching piano today but has the day off from Tsumiki.

"Hey, do you want to meet up during my lunch break and go shopping for swimsuits?" Mum says, shooting me an inquiring look over her coffee cup. "Your school-issued swim-suit won't do for the beach, will it?"

Maybe it's because she has really short hair, but Mum looks perfectly cool and comfortable in her white cotton sleeveless blouse in spite of the heat. And here I am, sweating like crazy, and the day's only just begun.

"I s'pose," I say, reluctantly.

"You suppose what?"

"I suppose I'll go."

"Okay then," Mum says, and smiles. "Meet me at the piano school right at noon sharp, all right?"

She drinks the last of her coffee and gets up. I nod and say okay.

I know it's not my place to worry, but I feel uneasy whenever Mum buys me something. Mum laughs and says that she makes enough money for us to get by on, and I know there's a savings account in my name. I know these things, but I still get nervous.

Mum keeps her money, her bankbook, and her official *inkan* name seal in a black evening clutch in case there's a fire or an earthquake so that she can just grab it if she needs to run. She says the Professor bought the bag for her. It's a really pretty velvet bag with lots of black beads on it.

"I don't think I'll be going to any more parties where I'll need this bag," she'd once said. When she did, she looked sad enough to make me shudder.

"I'm off," Mum says, ready to go. "Make sure you water the garden."

"Okay."

I watch Mum leave. I get a whiff of her usual scent, a mix of cigarettes, vanilla from her soap, and perfume.

"See you at noon."

I stand there for a while after the door closes behind her.

UBAGA POND

I wait for Soko to come home, my legs stretched out in front of me on the *tatami* mat, drinking an espresso. It's a Monday, my day off from work. The weeds in the garden are growing wild, and the late afternoon breeze carries the smell of soil through the screen door. Soko gets annoyed when I leave the sliding glass door open. The screen is torn in places and lets mosquitoes inside.

It's September. I close my eyes and feel the weak, setting sun on my eyelids.

"Escape? Where to?" I'd asked, and he said he didn't know. "Can't I go with you?" I asked again. He looked distraught.

"I'm sorry," I said. I didn't want to torment him. I didn't want to see him sad. It was a hot and humid evening. We were at Kitanomaru Park, and the smell of green was overwhelming. He held me tight. With his arms still wrapped around me, he gave a pained whisper that he was sorry. He suddenly let go, looked at me, and said, "I promise I'll be back." I promise to come back and find you, wherever you are, he said.

He had a wife and I had the Professor. His shop had been closed for a while, and he was in such dire straits, he said, that even debt collectors pitied him. There was nothing I could do as he told me all this with a weary smile. That was twelve years ago. I was twenty-five.

I get up and go to the kitchen, light a cigarette, and inhale. The kitchen is cool and dark, and I get a chill from the sudden change. The floor underneath my bare feet is cold and creaks heavily here and there. During the day, our house is awfully quiet.

It's past five, but Soko hasn't come home yet. Lately she's been getting home late all the time. I should probably be happy for her, since it means that she's made friends.

I turn on the radio, take a beer out of the fridge, and pop it open.

Yesterday, Mrs Oshita finished Burgmüller. The last piece was 'La Chevaleresque'. She got through its breezy tempo with her beautiful arms – thin and bony, covered in countless wrinkles and bumps, the skin sagging in complex shapes, with both dark and light brown spots – as she sat erect. Though she stumbled twice, her performance for the most part was rhythmical and extremely gratifying. I drew a circle on her sheet music and wrote "Fabulous!" on the side. Just like the Professor used to in my books.

Of course, the Professor rarely complimented me when I played the piano. In my four years in college, he only wrote that in my book twice.

✦ ✦ ✦

Straddling a bench made from half a tree trunk laid sideways on the ground, Numata-kun is playing 'Winterreise' on his recorder. His cheeks puff up with air, making his fair, round face even rounder. Because he's facing down, I can tell his eyelashes are really long. His fingertips are pressed against the holes of the recorder, and I can see that there's dirt underneath his nails, even though they're clipped short.

"I think you've improved a lot," I say when he's finished playing. "You'll probably pass next time."

Numata-kun lifts his gaze, and a look of genuine joy sweeps across his face. When he plays the recorder, though, he makes the most surprisingly sorrowful sounds.

Ever since summer ended and school started again, Numata-kun and I have been walking home together sometimes. We live in the same direction and neither of us go to cram schools or take any lessons after school. Plus, since our mums both work, no one's home even if we go straight home. So we hang out at Joshi Park, or kill time by Ubaga Pond, like today. Sometimes, Numata-kun's Mum treats us to cake at the museum coffee shop where she works.

At first, I would look away when I ran into Numata-kun at the museum, but we grew close over the course of the summer.

"How long have you been wearing grown-up clothes?" I asked him one day. It had been bothering me. That is, the gray, oversized trousers that he wears.

"Two years," he answered matter-of-factly, adding that he started wearing them in the last trimester of third grade.

"Does your Mum pick them out?"

"Uh-huh," he said, and nodded. He seemed not to care about his clothes or his body.

"You should wear something different," I worked up the courage to say. Numata-kun listened quietly. "There are other kinds of grown-up clothes, too, you know, like jeans and khakis."

His grey, baggy trousers are so noticeably odd. He doesn't fit in with our classmates at all. He looks like a middle-aged primary school pupil. He wears a grown-up belt, too, that makes him look even weirder.

I don't know whether he got it or not, but Numata-kun didn't appear to be the least bit offended, and it didn't seem like he had any intention of changing the way he dressed, either. He just had a vague smirk on his face.

It was the same with his homework. Two days before the end of summer vacation, I was shocked when Numata-kun told me that he hadn't done any of his homework.

"You haven't done *anything*?"

We'd been assigned a lot of homework.

"I'll show you my workbook. You should just copy off of me." He seemed uninterested when I told him I'd let him copy my homework, or when I offered to help him finish his assignments.

"No, it's okay," he said, and smirked. I was surprised, and then a bit impressed. It was something I could never do.

In the end, Numata-kun didn't turn in any of his homework. Because of all this, he sort of latched onto me once school started again.

"Do you want to go eat cake?" he asks as he puts his recorder in its case.

I shake my head. "Not today."

The setting sun is bouncing off the surface of Ubaga Pond. One of the things I like about Numata-kun is that at times like this, he doesn't ask why.

"Look!" I say, pointing my chin toward the small path leading to the history museum. There's a black cat walking along with a leisurely gait. The sun is shining on its fur.

I like late afternoon in this town.

When I get home, Mum is reading in the kitchen. She's wearing a dress made of soft, floppy material that's perfect for Mondays, when she doesn't work during the day.

"Hi," Mum says, raising her face from her book and smiling at me. There's a pile of cigarette butts in the ashtray.

"Do you remember Nana?" I ask all of a sudden. Nana's a cat that belonged to a neighbour in our building in Kawagoe.

"I saw a cat that looked exactly like Nana today. A really pretty black cat."

"You saw Nana?" Mum asks, with a frown. "Where?"

Mum liked Nana, too. She used to say that Nana's tiny tail was "endearing."

"At Ubaga Pond."

Mum falls silent and now it's my turn to frown.

"What, Mum? What's the matter?"

"Maybe she died," she says solemnly. I'm shocked.

"Why?!" I yell, in spite of myself.

Apparently, Mum had dreamt of Nana just this morning. In the dream, Nana was sleeping under the mailboxes at the entrance of the flat in Kawagoe, looking all cosy and content.

"It's already been two years since we left Kawagoe," Mum says, her eyes downcast. I stare at Mum, her short hair, her sharp chin. "But today was the first time I dreamt of Nana."

With absolute certainty in her voice, Mum says that Nana had probably come to say good-bye.

"That's the only reason why you think Nana died? Because she was in your dream?" I ask.

"And because you saw Nana on the same day," Mum says, as she puts a cigarette in her mouth and lights it.

"It wasn't Nana, it was just another cat that looked like Nana," I protest. But it's no use.

"It's all right," Mum says. "Nana lived a long life. And all animals that are loved in this life go to heaven."

I don't say anything because I just think that's weird. What about the animals that aren't loved, then? I don't ask, but that's what I'm thinking.

✦ ✦ ✦

By October, the air has become clear and autumnal. The summer's stubborn humidity has abated, and cigarettes and coffee taste far better than they used to.

Here, too, I go to work on my bike. Fall is when the pedals feel lightest.

I teach piano for two hours in the morning, shop, go home for lunch, and do laundry in the afternoon. Then I borrow Soko's Walkman and go for a walk.

The bank of the dry moat is steep, and I break into a run trying to walk down the hill. There are many large trees along the bank.

I like walking alone. When I'm alone I walk at a brisk pace, taking big steps. I keep walking, single-mindedly going onward. Sometimes when I walk, I'm overcome by an odd feeling. I may be walking just to get that feeling, although I don't experience it often. It's the feeling that my true love is suddenly walking toward me. It's a distinct feeling, not simply a figment of my imagination or wishful thinking. He appears and heads straight toward me all of a sudden.

If it really happened, I'd probably think, "well, of course." Not "why?" or "this can't be," but "of course." He'd be smiling. He'd have known that I'd be walking this way.

Neither of us would run toward each other. It would be as if every step that brought us closer were being carefully observed. As if, were we to take the wrong number of steps, or if our strides were too big or too small, we might suddenly disappear.

If I were to spot him beyond the dry moat where the grass has begun to wither, I wouldn't be the least bit surprised. I'd just think, "of course." Merely, "I've been waiting for you."

At first, I don't realize that someone's calling my name because I'm listening to music on the Walkman.

"Sensei!"

They must have been yelling to get my attention. I finally notice and look up to find Mrs Oshita and her husband.

"Oh." I hastily take my earphones off. "Hi, there. Are you taking a walk?" I bow to the elderly couple. They appear to have been walking along the flat part of the bank.

"Yes," Mrs Oshita beams. Her arm is wrapped around her husband's. "You, too?" It's a bit embarrassing to be called "sensei" by someone who's more than twice my age.

"Yes." I feel like a child, intimidated and taken aback. The sky is light blue, and the air is that of late afternoon.

We bow to each other again and go our respective ways. I watch the two of them walking together and feel a mild sense of loss. Of something that's gone from my life forever. Something that I've let go of.

"The immoral."

The expression comes to mind. He'd said that love was a privilege of the immoral. He may be right. But there are some places where immoral people can never go. This much I know, no matter how happy-go-lucky I may be. It's something I've never forgotten, not even for a moment.

After dinner, Soko sits close by and watches me as I prepare to go to work. She says she likes watching me get ready for work.

During the day, I stopped by a bookshop when I went shopping for groceries. Because I get all my books from the library, I rarely step foot inside bookshops. And when I do, I don't go to buy books, I go to browse music magazines like *Player*, *Guitar Magazine*, and *Jazz Life* that he used to have in his shop a long time ago. Magazines like *G.M. Square* and *Classified Bazaar* have pages for classified ads – from the genuinely serious to the comical – for those who want to sell or buy instruments, bands that are looking for vocalists, and people looking to make friends. If he were looking for me, I thought that maybe he'd place an ad. Though I can't be sure.

Just in case, I want to make sure I don't miss it. I read through ads like "Have an old Fender amplifier you don't need anymore?" or "Vintage Fender triple 8-string neck steel guitar with case available for 450,000 yen" or "Guitarist looking for drummer and bassist. Hoping to form a band that bounces off the walls at shows." or "Looking for people to go to gigs with." Every month there's ad after ad, all of which sound pretty much the same. I check them all, just in case.

Years ago when I first left Tokyo, I placed ads in some of the magazines. There was "To the owner of the music store Pasado. Please get in touch." And "Looking for the Narcisco Yepes recording that begins with introductions and variations on a theme of Mozart and ends with 'Juegos Prohibidos.'" He'd made me a tape of that recording once.

Though he was forced to close his shop because he could no longer keep the business afloat, I can't imagine him doing anything not related to music, which is why I thought it might be possible he's reading these magazines. If he'd seen my ads – if only he'd seen my ads – everything would have worked out.

I got some responses to the ads, but none of them were serious.

"Why don't you ever wear pink?" Soko asks me as I put on my lipstick. "Pink lipstick would be cute."

Soko likes pink.

"You know, like the lipstick Maho in Takahagi used to wear?"

I screw up my face and meet Soko's eyes in the mirror to let her know how I feel about the suggestion.

"Do you not like pink?"

"It doesn't look good on me." I only wear red lipstick.

"Hmm," Soko says, with a look of displeasure.

The bar manager makes me a dish of fried *udon* just as I'm about to make myself some coffee. It's not on the menu, but it's a specialty of his that he'll make if any of our customers request it. He makes it with cabbage, carrot, and corned beef.

"This is delicious." I'm not trying to flatter him; it's delicious.

"It goes really well with wine," the manager says, reaching into the fridge for a bottle of white wine and pouring me a glass.

"You're spoiling me," I say jokingly, and he shrugs. He's wearing his signature black polo shirt.

"I don't do this for just anyone."

"Thank you," I say. And that should be the end of it. Both the manager and I are old enough to know how to read between the lines – or to read between the lines and ignore what's there.

"I'll leave you to lock up, then," he says, and leaves through the back door.

The bar is quiet after the "closed" sign is hung on the door. With half the lights turned off, the shadows and smells of the customers who had just left linger in the air, and it makes me feel lonely. I wash the dishes, tie up the rubbish bag, and haul it out into the street.

A BONE-MELTING LOVE AFFAIR

Christmas is fun. After dinner, Mum and I eat an entire strawberry shortcake by ourselves. It's covered in so much whipped cream – the kind of cake Mum would never buy on a regular day. But we finish the whole thing. We split it into four pieces, two for each of us.

"Why do we do something special for Christmas?" I ask.

"It doesn't really matter what the excuse is," Mum says as she shoves cake into her mouth. "The important thing is that we have them. Like birthdays and Christmas."

"Hmm," I say. Still unconvinced, I ask, "Why?"

Mum opens her eyes wide, pretending to be surprised.

"Isn't it more fun that way?" Her expression says, "Don't ask me such obvious questions." She takes another bite of cake and lets out a satisfied grunt.

"Look at this white, fluffy cream with its brilliant sweetness and vegetable shortening in all its glory!"

I laugh. Mum looks happy, even as she knocks the cake.

"It's kind of exciting to eat something that's bad for you," Mum says apologetically.

Mum plays a few Christmas songs on the piano. I like songs with beautiful, melancholy melodies like 'Gabriel's Message' and 'Do You Hear What I Hear?' Mum, though, likes more upbeat ones like 'Have Yourself A Merry Little Christmas' and 'Winter Wonderland' – in her words, "songs that have a bright and warm feel to them." I stand beside her as she plays the piano and watch how her strong fingers move with unbelievable flexibility.

After our bath, we talk about Dad. About how things would be if Dad were around. That's what Mum and I like to talk about when we're both in a really good mood. About what Dad would do if he were here.

"He'd kiss me!" I say. This is what Mum always used to say first, and now it's become a race of who can say it before the other.

"Yes, he'd give you kisses," Mum says, slowly. "You couldn't escape him. He'd kiss every part of you. Even your eyelids and your wrist and your belly button."

It makes me happy and I can't help giggling.

"He'd make me a grass whistle."

We keep going.

"He'd let me use his arm as a pillow."

That's Mum. We keep adding things to the list as they come to us. He'd go on walks with us. He'd drive away bad dreams. He'd make delicious, frosty cocktails. He'd let us touch his shapely forehead and beautiful calves. He'd teach us how to swim and play tennis. He'd take us to a batting cage. He'd hold us. He'd greet us in the morning when we wake up. He'd let us know that we're not two lonely girls all on our own. He'd be here forever.

Even after we get under our covers, we keep adding more to the list. He'd eat ice cream with us. He'd let us draw his portrait. He'd take us to Paris. He's let us comb his hair.

Mum and I don't give each other presents for Christmas. We don't decorate our house. Instead, we talk about Dad, feel a little happier, and fall into a deep sleep.

The new year came around, and then, the beginning of the third trimester. I like the last trimester the best, because it's short and I've got used to stuff – to all kinds of things – by then. I hate the first trimester of school, when everything is still new.

I think getting used to things is really important. Though Mum gave me a funny look when I once told her that.

✦ ✦ ✦

"A bucket?" the bar manager asks from across the counter as he sips whiskey with water along with some of our regular customers.

"Yes, a bucket," I nod, to which one of the regular says, "What a great idea," and laughs. My hands and feet are always cold, so I soak my feet in a bucket of hot water when I read. I'm explaining this to the customers as I pour them whiskey with water.

"The water cools pretty fast, so I keep a thermos nearby. That way, I can keep adding more hot water to the bucket."

"Yoko, you're quite a character." The customers laugh again.

"It keeps me warm and feels quite nice."

It's January, and it's especially cold out tonight. An icy gust of air rushes into the bar every time someone opens the door. The smell of winter, clinging to customers' coats, makes its way inside.

"I prefer that women be somewhat vulnerable to the cold, actually," a middle-aged customer bordering on old age says. "Women who are always complaining about being too hot seem rather immodest to me."

I laugh inside. What an inane thing to say. But the Professor used to say something similar.

The Professor didn't like it when my skin was exposed. He used to say that in the summer, it was cooler to keep yourself covered up when going out. It was true. I learned a lot of things from him, like how it's better to have something hot to drink in the heat instead of something cold, and that it's more effective to warm up your feet than wear extra layers when you're cold.

But there were a lot of things he didn't know, like the names of common plants, different kinds of delicious junk food, or the fact that everyday spiders and geckos are harmless.

At times, the Professor was like a child. Whenever he was served something he didn't recognize in a restaurant, he frowned.

"What might this be?" he'd ask me, uneasily. Since I'm not afraid to eat anything, I'd always try things first. Then I'd tell him that they were crushed pistachios, or that I thought it might be minced fish, and his expression would soften a bit. Still doubtful, though, he'd mutter, "I wonder if it's all right to eat?"

Only after I'd reassured him that "of course, it's fine" would he finally eat, completely confident in my assertion. It just broke my heart. Why did this man trust me so completely? It made me want to cry.

He was a sweet man. I was happy with him.

But now, I'm here.

"I'd like some shochu with hot water. Drop a sour plum in it, too," the ageing customer says.

When I get home, Soko is sleeping, flanked on both sides by her dolls. She's matured a lot lately, but her sleeping routine hasn't changed. I climb under the covers with my clothes still on, hold Soko from behind, and kiss the top of her head. Soko squirms and says, "You're cold." Ever loyal to our routine, Soko endearingly adds, "Welcome home." She lets me hold my cold cheek against hers.

"I'm home." I rub my cheek against hers, my heart bursting with love.

✦ ✦ ✦

It's Sunday, and it's sunny outside. Mum's been in a good mood since this morning. She says the book she checked out yesterday from the library is really good, and has been reading it all day.

"What's it about?" I ask.

"I can't tell you in a nutshell," is all she says. Then, probably feeling a bit guilty, she adds, "It's a mystery novel."

Mum gets caught up really easily. She seems unaware that the washing machine has stopped, so I hang the laundry out to dry.

In the afternoon I'm bored, and I go for a walk by myself. Going straight down the street between the middle school and high school, I head for Joshi Park. It's the route Mum and I always take on our walks. There's a dry wind, strong and icy. At times like this, Mum takes the scarf she wears around her neck and wraps it around her head and face. I tell her not to because it's embarrassing, but she won't listen.

"But it's warmer this way," she insists, explaining that comfort is what's most important. "Stop worrying about what other people think," she says. But when I keep nagging her, she shoots off a curt, "Stop being so ridiculous!" leaving no more room for discussion.

"Stop being so ridiculous!" I imitate Mum out loud, all alone on the winter road.

I sit on the dead grass by the dry moat under the blue sky. I lie on my back and watch the clouds beyond the branches of the trees. When I turn my head to the side, the dry, overgrown grass prickles my cheek.

I sit up and take my nail-filing kit out of my bag. Mum bought it for me the other day at the drugstore.

On the bank, I polish my nails. I can hear a helicopter in the sky high above me. I take Allie out of my bag, too, and sit her next to me.

Long ago, my mum had a love affair passionate enough to melt bones.

Who knows what that means, but regardless, I was the result of the love affair.

"It would be great if someday, the same wonderful thing happens to you, too," Mum's said to me several times. And every time, she rephrases what she's said, apologetically. "Well, there's no way the exact same thing could happen, but at least something like it."

I put away my nail-filing kit and admire my hands with satisfaction. Each nail is shiny, and they feel nice and smooth when I rub them.

"The same thing won't happen?" I ask.

"Well, there's only one man like your father in the entire world," Mum says in a dreamy voice, but with absolute certainty. I sometimes think that Mum is cuckoo. When it comes to Dad, she's totally nuts.

A lady and her dog walk by. The lady's wearing a mask and gloves. Why is it that the more layers people wear, the colder they look? The dog is a Shiba with a red collar. I can hear him pressing his nose against the ground, his paws treading on the dead grass and dirt.

When I was a lot younger, I used to believe that I'd meet Dad someday. That even as we went about our lives he was looking for us, and that one day he would surely find us.

I pull up my socks, stand up, and brush the grass off my bottom. I need to head home soon. Mum gets worried when I get home too late. I bend over and pick Allie up, brush the dirt off her, and put her back in my bag.

When I get home, it smells like coffee. There's a pair of men's shoes – worn-out bit loafers – by the front door. They put me in a bad mood. I go inside without saying anything.

"Hey, you're back," Mum says cheerfully when she sees me. She's drinking coffee at the kitchen table.

"Hello." It's the manager of Tsumiki. He's wearing a black sweater, white trousers, and white socks.

"Hello." I greet him back with a sulky look – the one that Mum calls my "stony face." There's a box of Godiva chocolates on the table, which I know Mum doesn't like that much.

"What happened to the book?" I ask, and Mum looks confused.
"The book?"

"The thriller. The one you were buried in since yesterday."

"Oh," Mum says, and smiles. "I finished it."

She lights a cigarette and blows smoke through her lips.

"Look," Mum says, and shows me a folded blanket. It's a pretty, baby-blue blanket. "The manager gave it to me."

From the way she says this and the way she casually plucks the blanket from the table with the same hand that's holding her cigarette, I can tell she's not too thrilled about it.

"Hmm," I respond, my mood lifting somewhat. I think Mum can tell. We're the meanest mother-daughter pair in the entire world, for sure.

"I figured a blanket is more convenient than hot water in a bucket, and safer, too." The bar manager looks happy.

✦ ✦ ✦

As a child, I often drank hot cocoa on winter nights. My mother would make it for me herself. Her cocoa was thick and hot, and would nearly burn my lips no matter how careful I was. She made the cocoa in a small pan, and said the key to making good cocoa was to stir it thoroughly at the beginning, and to add just a pinch of salt at the end. But since the cocoa I make for Soko is from an instant mix, I just add boiling milk to the cup with a packet of powder.

Soko still enjoys it, though. She says it's better than any other cocoa she's had.

"That manager's just weird," Soko says, holding her cup of cocoa with both her hands. She's sitting on the *tatami* mat floor with her legs stretched out in front of her.

"What do you mean, 'weird?'"

"Well, why did he come all the way to our house?"

"I suppose that was strange," I say.

"And he's too skinny."

Soko's ruthless.

"That's not a nice thing to say," I say like a mother should, but Soko is unfazed.

"I know you think so, too."

I put my lips against Soko's shiny hair, appealing to her to stop.

When Soko was still a baby, I always kissed her twice.

"This is from me. And this one's from Dad," I'd say.

But I soon stopped. Because there's only person in the world who can kiss the way he does.

I open the window and lean out into the garden.

"The stars are beautiful. Look, there are so many of them."

Without even a perfunctory glance, Soko says that she's too cold. I regret not knowing anything about stars. I wish I could teach Soko the constellations – that's Orion, that's the North Star – the way my mother used to teach me. The way he would teach her, if only he were here.

"Come on, I'm cold," Soko says, and quickly closes the window.

"You're not much of a romantic," I say.

Widening her eyes on purpose as if in exasperation, Soko says, "You're *too* much of a romantic, Mum."

"Well, excuse me," I say. For a while, we sit without talking. The radio is turned down but still on in the kitchen, playing a recent pop song I can't comprehend.

"Yo says she's going to become Topo Gigio."

I was sitting on my father's lap, a seat reserved just for me. He smelled distinctly like himself – my father.

"You're a funny girl, Yoko," my mother said, amused. It made me happy that my words brought joyful laughter to my parents.

February is here, and I'm thirty-eight years-old. Thirty-eight. It's mind-boggling.

"I can't believe you're really going." The day I left on my journey, my mother cried. "It's insane. Leaving with nowhere to go, with a baby to take care of."

My father said nothing. He looked sad, but he probably knew it was no use trying to stop me.

"Yo says she's going to become Topo Gigio."

Sometimes I so badly want them to meet Soko.

It's February.

The daphnes in the garden have bloomed. When I step into the garden early in the morning, I'm overpowered by their scent. There's a light frost on the windows, and the cold pierces my fingertips when I rub them against the glass. Wearing only a pair of thin socks, the *tatami* mat feels terrifyingly cold against my feet.

AUTUMN BREEZE

Once you cross paths with someone, you can never lose them.

For example, even though my true love is not here with me, I can imagine what it would be like if he were. I can imagine what he would say, what he would do. Just envisioning these things has saved me on numerous occasions. Given me the courage to do what I need to do.

It's been almost twelve years since I left Tokyo. Like my mother once said, what I've done is probably not something anyone in her right mind would do. But both Soko and I are well, each year we age another year, and spend our days working, sleeping, entering swimming meets. For twelve years, I haven't had contact with anyone in Tokyo. Not the Professor, of course, nor the few friends I had, my father, my mother, my cousins.

Cutting everyone off was much easier than I'd expected. All I had to do was pretend they didn't exist. That none of them had ever existed, and that I had no place to return to. If it weren't for this self-deception, there's no way Soko and I could have managed on our own.

It's August, our second summer in Sakura. The thriving weeds in our garden have grown tall again this year, and their pungent smell is overwhelming in the evenings when there's no breeze.

The *tatami* mats, faded from green to amber, feel damp, maybe because I walk on them in my bare feet. They creak with every step I take.

At one in the afternoon I make some cold *somen* noodles for myself, and when I'm finished with them, eat a mandarin orange. The wind chimes clink in the light breeze.

The manager at the bar gave me the mandarin oranges. They were apparently a gift from a customer. Summer oranges are small with thin rinds, and almost painfully sweet.

Lately, I've been loath to go to work. The manager has been too nice. I'm not good at dealing with nice men.

I throw out the orange peel in the garbage can, wipe my fingertips on a kitchen towel, and lie on my stomach on the *tatami* mat. My neck is stiff and my hands and feet feel heavy. It's the heat and humidity. I think about moving.

Soko and I played with sparklers last night.

We bought a variety pack at a convenience store nearby. We lit them in our garden that's overrun with weeds, both of us in our rubber flip-flops. The darkness of the late-summer night was thick. Insects were singing, and because it had rained earlier in the evening, the smell of wet soil filled the air.

"Such beautiful bones," I said, as I looked at Soko's back. Her spine really looks so much like his. It's not that I can actually see her bones, of course, but I know what's there beyond her warmth, on the other side of her skin.

"Your hair's grown." I caressed Soko's soft hair.

"Don't you think sparklers have a fierce smell?" Soko asked.

"Fierce?" I thought it was a weird expression to use for sparklers, but since Soko looked so serious, I merely agreed. "You're right."

A long time ago, the Professor and I often played with sparklers. I spent numerous summers with him. The Professor was clumsy and had trouble lighting the candle we used to start our sparklers. Crouching on the sidewalk and praying there'd be no gusts of wind, we'd rush to light our sparklers one after another, checking now and again to see how the other was doing. It was more important to me that the Professor was enjoying himself than to have fun myself, and likewise, he genuinely wanted to show me a good time.

Soko's slender legs stretched straight out from her shorts. The sparkler in her hand cast a light on her thighs and shins.

"The smell of sparklers clings to your memory, doesn't it?" I said to Soko, recalling the expression on the Professor's face as he struggled to light the candle.

◆　◆　◆

"You're good at everything," Numata-kun says, with a helpless look on his face. We're drinking cream sodas at the coffee shop in the museum. The other side of the glass window is flooded with sunlight. It's summer, and nothing much is going on.

"What do you mean, 'everything'?"

"You get good marks, you're good at music and art. Maybe you're not that good in P.E., but you still passed level three in swimming."

Numata-kun is wearing a white tank top, grey trousers, and white trainers. He looks like a timid middle-aged man, but has a rather childish face.

"That doesn't mean anything," I say. We've been talking about clubs and committees for next semester. I'm in the gardening club, and switch committees every semester. Numata-kun hasn't joined any clubs, and he always gets stuck with something pathetic like the cleaning committee, which means you have to stay after school to write up "cleaning reports" even when you're not on cleaning duty, or the animal care committee, even though he doesn't like animals.

"You decide what you want to do and run for the position. That's all it takes."

Numata-kun looks at a loss, and shrugs.

"Well, you're good at everything," he says once more, in a tiny, weak voice.

When I get home, Mum's taking a nap on the *tatami* mat. There's a book lying face down next to her, and further away sits a bowl of *somen* noodles (I can tell because there's cloudy water in it) and a small dipping bowl. The radio in the kitchen is on.

"Hi, Mum." I put my bags down and carry the bowls to the kitchen. A postcard I sent Mum from my three-day school trip to Nikko last month is stuck to the fridge with a magnet. It's the first postcard I've ever sent her.

We went to Nikko by bus. Mum says she gets excited about buses, but I don't like them that much, probably because I get carsick. I don't like the exhaust-filled air at rest stops, either.

There's a photo of a waterfall on the postcard. In the photo, there's lots of water spilling down the waterfall. The one I actually saw looked completely different.

"Hi, honey," Mum says hoarsely as she comes into the kitchen. "It's hot, isn't it? I hope you remembered to wear a hat when you went out."

Mum takes some iced barley tea out of the refrigerator, pours just half a small cupful and drinks it. "Did you get a lot of homework done?"

I've told her that I go to the museum to do my homework.

"Yeah, I guess," I say. Good, Mum says, puts a cigarette between her lips, and lights it. She exhales a wisp of smoke. The English news is on the radio.

✦ ✦ ✦

It's a slow day at the bar again today. The manager is roasting a pond herring, and a customer is telling a story about his golf score finally breaking 80. I think bars should go on vacation in the summers, too, like the piano school where I work. But the manager would probably smile silently and say that he'd have nothing to do if he closed the bar, but, "Of course, you should feel free to take more days off, though."

"Do you play golf?" the customer asks me, and I shake my head.

"I'm no good at sports."

It's a quiet night. At Tsumiki, there's a small window with light green curtains. The manager's ex-wife made them.

"I hear you were in Ibaraki before you moved here," says the customer, who is tan and has a receding hairline.

"Yes, in Takahagi."

"Hmm," he says, and takes a sip of his whiskey and water.

"And before that?"

"Kawagoe."

The manager adds that I'd been working at a bar in Kawagoe owned by an acquaintance of his. Hmm, the customer says again.

"Where are you originally from?"

"Tokyo," I answer, and bring my glass of iced oolong tea to my lips. The cold glass has been sitting for a while and is wet with condensation.

"Hmm. So you've had some drama in your past, huh?"

"Well, I guess," I say, and smile. "Drama" is such a strange expression. It sounds like things are really complicated. But my "drama" isn't complicated at all. It's all very simple.

What can you do though, I think, as I recall his eyes the first time I ever met him. What can you do? There's no way anyone could understand. There's no way anyone could understand, but my "drama" is all in those eyes.

✦ ✦ ✦

The new semester has started, but the heat hasn't let up at all. Numata-kun was assigned to the cleaning committee again after all. He accepted the position with a ridiculous smile on his face.

I won second place among sixth graders for my summer art homework, a drawing I did of Joshi Park. As usual, Mum hugged me tight. She said, "You're even artistically talented."

I can hear the rain hitting the window. It's been raining every day lately. Mum's been reading for a while tonight. Wednesday night at our house.

"Why don't you go ahead and take a bath?" Mum says, without raising her eyes from her book.

"Mm-hm," I answer half-heartedly.

When I was little, I hated rainy nights. They made me feel like Mum was never going to come home, as I lay all alone in my futon.

"Can I play the piano for a little bit?" I ask. Mum nods.

"Just one piece, though, because it's late."

I open the lid of the piano.

Whenever I got scared on those rainy nights, I used to think about Dad. I thought about him in my futon, with Allie and the pink bear lying next to me.

If only Dad were here with me. If only he would take me in his arms, a place Mum says is heavenly. If only he would show me that smile on his beautiful face. If only he would lend me the hollow beneath his shoulders that fit Mum's cheekbones perfectly, just for a little bit.

When I thought about Dad, the sound of raindrops hitting the roof grew distant. And when the sound of the rain grew softer, I was able to sleep. That's when I was really little.

"Gluck?"

I notice that Mum's standing by the piano now. Gavotte Von Gluck is a piece in *Piano Pieces with Ferdinand Beyer, Part 2*.

"The sounds you make on the piano are so soft," Mum says, and brings her lips to my head. Her scent wafts gently toward me.

"Will you play just one piece?" I ask.

Mum reaches for the sheet music. "Any requests?"

"Bach." Without question. Mum plays a short mass. It's short, but so strikingly beautiful.

"Isn't Bach great?" I say.

When I get out of the bath, Mum is still reading. Even after I drink my milk, brush my teeth, and get under the covers, she's still reading.

"Aren't you coming to bed yet?" I say from my futon.

"I want to read just a bit more."

Mum is engrossed in her book. I think about the Professor, the man who loved Mum. It's weird, but sometimes I feel like it's easier to think about the Professor than about Dad. The man who fell in love with Mum, married her, and watched as Dad took her away.

Of course, Mum gets upset when I put it that way. She says she's never been "taken" away by anyone or "taken" anyone away.

Mum has really fair skin. Because of her short hair, her pale neck is always exposed. She's skinny, and her collarbones form hollows on her neck so deep that puddles form when she showers. The hands that hold her books as she reads are big and sinewy. They're a piano player's hands, she says. The hands that always squeeze my head tight. The same hands that probably held the Professor's head and Dad's head now turn the pages of the thick book – a mystery, probably – that she's reading.

"Good night," I say, as I look at her.

"Good night," Mum says, returning my gaze.

✦ ✦ ✦

In October, the sky definitely seems to stretch higher than before, more intensely blue and clear.

I shuffle the hem of my skirt around as I walk aimlessly. I'm listening to Rod Stewart.

I feel completely at a loss. I haven't been so utterly overwhelmed in a long time.

This morning, I floated the idea of moving again because the weather was beautiful and I was feeling good.

"I knew this was coming soon," Soko said without a hint of surprise. "When?"

She was having her usual breakfast of cereal, eggs, and tea.

"Next year."

I was staring at Soko from the side as I drank coffee from a big mug. Her small nose, her soft lips, and the forehead that looks just like his.

"I'm thinking around spring," I said, as I rested a cheek in one hand and stared harder at Soko.

"Where to?"

Soko starts junior high next spring.

"Hmm, I don't know yet. I'm hoping somewhere near the ocean. Is there anywhere you want to go?"

"Not really," Soko said. She seemed quite upset.

"Do you want to stay here longer?" I asked. "Do you like it here in Sakura?"

"Forget it."

Holding her cereal bowl with both hands, Soko drank the leftover milk.

"Are you sad about leaving your friends?"

"Forget it," she said, yet again.

"No matter where you go, they'll always be your friends, right?"

Soko glared. She wouldn't even answer me.

I could tell who she was thinking about. Rikako had been Soko's best friend in Takahagi, and they wrote each other for a while after we moved to Sakura. But somewhere along the line, they'd lost touch.

"Rikako, even…" I began, going out on a limb. "I don't think the fact that Rikako is your friend has changed. Or at least that she was your friend."

Facts don't disappear. Which means we never feel loss. That's all I wanted Soko to understand.

"I know," Soko said. "But it all disappears into the box, right?"

She didn't sound convinced.

"Why do I have to put everything in the box? Why do we have to move all the time? Why can't we just wait for Dad here?"

"I've told you. You and I are birds of passage." I knew this was a weak argument. Soko's eyes were pleading for a better explanation. Her entire body seemed to declare that she no longer wanted to keep going.

"I feel like I'll never see him again if I settle down somewhere," I offer honestly, because I have no other choice.

"So, if you don't settle down somewhere, you'll see him again? Do you really believe that?"

I was floored.

"Of course," I said, but now I knew that Soko didn't believe it. "Why do you think we won't?" I lit a cigarette. My fingers were shaking.

"I don't know."

Soko's voice was terribly soft. Soon, unable to bear it any longer, she began to sob. "I'm sorry," she said. "I'm sorry I said we won't see Dad again."

My heart sank at that moment. If I'd tried to say anything, I think I would've cried. I snuffed my cigarette on an ashtray and finished off my coffee.

What would he do at a time like this? I raise the volume of Rod Stewart's voice and forge ahead as if to erase the loneliness.

I want to see the water, so I walk to Inba Marsh. The water sparkles as it flows from the river into the marsh, and there's a middle-aged man fishing by himself on the embankment. The red windmill is still, as usual.

I stand in the autumn breeze.

"Do you really think that you're going to be able to manage on your own?" my mother had said that morning, in a tone that was hard to tell whether she was scolding me or trying to stop me from going. "Do you seriously believe you can manage on your own as a single mother?"

My mother, a great seamstress, had a large mouth and was a big fan of Glenn Gould. My mother, who kept my father company for his nightcaps almost every night, and wore Mitsouko perfume when she went out. My mother, whom I left behind.

When I found out I was pregnant with Soko, there was no question in my mind. I knew right away that it was my third gift. My third and most precious gift.

"Why do we have to move all the time?"

How should I have answered her? There's a chilly wind by the water, and I rub my arms through the sleeves of my blouse.

"Do you really believe you'll see him again?"

The water in the marsh is muddy. There's algae growing in it, and disintegrating cigarette butts float on the surface. The water is leaden and cloudy and doesn't move at all, unaffected by the beautiful weather. Several wooden boats have been abandoned in the water. They're half rotten and broken, and look like they could sink at any moment.

I remember Soko's warmth and touch when she was little, clinging to my leg.

I remember her in the breeze.

ZUSHI, 2001

When Mum first met Dad, she was twenty-three years old and Dad was twenty-six.

Apparently, Dad told Mum, "If we'd met in elementary school, there's no way I would've let you get that scar on your shoulder."

"If we'd met in middle school, we would've run far away from home together."

"If we'd met in high school, I would've played the guitar for you every day."

"If we'd met in college, neither you nor I would be here right now."

But that's not how things actually worked out, so Mum had a scar on her shoulder from a fight, and she ran away from home alone one day when she was in middle school. In high school, she had cotton candy-coloured hair and went out dancing by herself every day. And because all the stuff Dad said wouldn't happen did happen, she's here right now.

Zushi is a city with lots of trees.

Whenever we walk along the broad, tree-lined streets with the huge houses, Mum exclaims, "It's just like Beverly Hills."

Two months have passed since we moved here. Last month, I started middle school.

The middle school is right by a Shinto shrine. There's a cuckoo clock on the first floor of the big, new gym.

"That's great," Mum said, when I told her about it. "So when you're exercising, a bird comes out and gives you the time."

That's not exactly how it works. The cuckoo clock is in the lobby right by the entrance, which is sectioned off from the actual gym by a heavy door, so we can't see or hear the clock during gym. Everyone pretty much forgets it exists. But I like the clock anyway, and that's what matters.

The day before our move, Mum and I had our "last supper" in a room full of moving boxes in the shabby flat with a garden in Sakura, where we'd lived for two years.

Since I was graduating from elementary school, I didn't have to suffer through a going-away party. But some of my friends gave me cards. For some reason, an old lady who took piano lessons from Mum gave me a handkerchief, even though we'd never met. She gave Mum a handbag.

"This was a nice city," Mum said, as we ate our meal. She said it flat-out in the past tense, and there was no trace of doubt in her smile. It's always this way. She never questions her decisions.

Just a little while before she offered her impression of Sakura, though, Mum said, "We don't have to move if you don't want to. If you want to stay here a little bit longer, we will."

I don't know. I don't know how long "a little bit longer" would have been, what would have happened had we stayed there, and why I said that I'd move. I don't know.

The only things I do know are that we are birds of passage, and that Mum believes in "God's boat."

I said good-bye to Numata-kun near Ubaga Pond. He wasn't surprised. Or at least, he didn't show it.

"Huh," he said, as if he wanted to say, "I knew it," and looked at the pond.

"Take care," I said.

He nodded and simply said, "What can you do? Parents have their reasons." He was wearing his baggy grey grown-up trousers.

He didn't say that we should meet up again sometime or that he'd write me letters. Both Numata-kun and I knew that we'd never see each other again.

When we moved to Zushi, Mum bought a scooter. It's a small, navy-blue one that suits her well. She rides it to work every day. She climbs onto it wearing a navy-blue helmet, red lipstick, and a flowy skirt. She says it's "very fast and very comfortable."

Mum and I take a lot of walks here, too. Usually we go to the beach, but sometimes we walk toward the station and have cake at a coffee shop.

✦ ✦ ✦

The sand at Zushi beach is the colour of the sand you find in sandboxes. Dark grey and heavy-looking. Where it's wet, it's black.

Clouds hang low in the sky.

"Hull" apparently refers to the body of a ship. I found out last night from the owner of Hull, the restaurant-slash-café-slash-bar where I've been working for the past month. It's run by a married couple who are into yachts.

"At sea, we use the term 'hull-down' to refer to something that's far away," he said. "It means that a yacht or a ship is so far away that you can see the mast, but not the hull."

As I walk down the beach, I strain my eyes and look far out into the ocean. The horizon is a hazy grey. There's nothing visible hull-down. It's a quiet afternoon.

Last month, I went to Soko's entrance ceremony at her middle school. I'm not a big fan of schools so I was a bit nervous, but Soko seemed nice and relaxed. I suppose this move has probably been less nerve-wracking than switching schools in the middle of the school year. Not that I've checked with her to see if that's really the case.

I felt funny watching Soko in her new uniform, and her green school shoes with blue stripes. Soko – our Soko – is wearing a peculiar outfit, I thought. It made me want to reclaim her.

"Don't be ridiculous."

That's what he would've said, laughing, I told myself while trying to exercise restraint. Even though I hate holding myself back.

I walk up the sandy beach, climb over the guardrail, and light a cigarette. From the road, I take in the view of the beach.

There's no one on the beach in May. There's just a carpenter working silently on the frame of a beach hut.

✦ ✦ ✦

When I get home from school, Mum is baking a chocolate cake. The cake is one of Mum's specialties; the chocolate is really rich, and it's delicious. When we lived in Soka, we often brought some over for the old lady next door.

"Hi, honey." Mum, reading in the kitchen, kisses the top of my head. The kitchen is filled with the sounds from the radio and the smell of baking cake.

"Look," Mum says as she shows me the spine of her book. There's a library sticker on it.

"You found a library?" Soon after we move to a new place, Mum starts looking for libraries. "How was it?"

"Convenient, it's right by the station." Mum adds that it's small but seems to have a pretty good selection of books. "The librarians seem nice, too."

I take off my uniform and hang it on the head jamb of the sliding door. I wash my hands and gargle.

The two-floor wooden flat is painted white, and is a fifteen-minute walk from my school. "It's awfully girly," Mum had said when the estate agent showed us the flat.

"I stopped by the beach after I went to the library. It was calm, no wind," she says.

Mum likes the ocean, even though she can't swim. I can swim a little bit, but I don't like the ocean very much.

A few days ago, a girl in my class told me I look like my mum. She said she'd seen her at the entrance ceremony. "You look exactly the same," is what she'd said. It seemed weird to me because I don't think we look alike at all.

Mum tells me I resemble her cousin, Mihoko, both in the way I'm "level-headed and reliable" and have "a look of determination."

Mihoko gave Mum a backpack as a present when I was born. Not baby clothes, not a terry cloth doll, but a backpack for carrying nappies and bottles. Mum says "it's so very typical of her – practical and considerate" to have come up with such a gift.

After dinner, Mum and I have chocolate cake and coffee. We're having espresso, and Mum laughs at me when I add milk. Milk with espresso is funny, apparently. She learned that from the Professor.

But I don't care. Mum taught me that it's stupid to care about what other people think.

"Are you enjoying your lessons?" Mum asks. I just nod yes. Mum says she's glad.

✦ ✦ ✦

I'm not a morning person, especially on sunny days like today. I hear the rustling of a plastic bag in the kitchen. It's Soko's job to take the bins out.

I reach for the pack of cigarettes by my pillow. After slowly smoking a cigarette, I forcibly peel myself away from my futon and take a shower.

Thanks to my PIANO LESSONS sign, I now have three students. One is a five-year-old, and the other two are housewives. Going out for lessons doesn't seem to be a common practice around here, so I visit my students' homes to give lessons instead. (It's one of the reasons I bought a scooter.)

After I see Soko off, I do a brisk clean of the flat, quickly get dressed, take my time warming up my fingers, and set off for work.

"I'm thinking of teaching piano."

When I told the Professor, he was silent for just a brief moment.

Then, "I think that's a good idea," he'd said. "I think you'd be good at it. Playing the piano and teaching piano are two completely different things, but music school graduates far less talented than you have been known to take students."

"That's not a very nice thing to say," I said. But I knew it was true.

Thinking back, maybe there was some irony to the situation. The woman who was about to leave the Professor was trying to make a living from the piano, which he had taught her.

The Professor played the piano with such precision. Precision and control that somehow made it all the more sensual.

It's early summer. I put on my helmet, lock the door, and leave the flat.

When I told the manager at Tsumiki that I would have to quit because I was moving, he looked hesitant. By that, I mean he looked like he was both surprised and confused.

"I'm sorry, especially since you've been so kind to me," I apologised.

"When are you going?" The manager looked increasingly troubled. Such an honest person, I thought.

"Not yet. Not until Soko graduates," I replied, and smiled. I knew how important it was to smile. It was a gesture letting him know that my mind was already made up.

It was January. We'd just closed the bar after a slow day and were putting the stools on the counter.

"It's going to sting, losing a hard worker like you."

"You'll find someone new before long," I assured him with confidence. The manager didn't respond.

After some time, he detachedly said, "I probably won't hire anyone new for a while," as if it were someone else's problem. "It's not so big a place that I can't manage it by myself."

He fluttered his eyes, which looked like mere lines on his face. He was wearing his trademark black polo shirt. "Where are you moving to?" he asked, brightly.

Relieved, I said, "Kanagawa."

"Kanagawa, huh?" he said, smiling.

Word-of-mouth is a very powerful medium.

After a lesson in the morning, I'm sitting in the restaurant where we'd agreed to meet. I'm surrounded by four women.

The interior of the restaurant, which serves southern French cuisine, has striking, warm yellow walls and wooden tables. One can enjoy a generously portioned lunch here for just 2,000 yen.

I'm kind of nervous and leave most of every course on my plate, enough that one of my lunch companions, a married woman whom I suspect is in her mid-thirties, says, "You eat like a bird." Her hair is always perfectly coiffed, and she wears feminine blouses with puffy sleeves.

The women talk a lot. And in between, they eat a lot. They smell of perfume and leave smudges of lipstick on the rims of their wine glasses.

In a daze, I smoke cigarette after cigarette. I feel like I'm in the wrong place, a feeling I've always had. When I was in college, in high school – and even back in elementary school – I'd had the same feeling.

The three women all want to take piano lessons. Two of the three played the piano as children. All three are married, and two of them have small children.

"But it won't be a problem, because you're willing to come to our homes to give us lessons," says the woman with the puffy sleeves.

"I want to play Erik Satie someday," says the woman with the glasses, who says she took piano lessons until she graduated from middle school.

I run out of cigarettes, and anxiously sip my espresso.

"Three people?" Soko says, her eyes popping with amazement. "All of a sudden you have three more students?"

Our Sunday morning walks have become routine since we moved to Zushi. We take about half an hour to walk through the neighborhood.

"That means you'll make more money," Soko says.

The house with the lilies is Soko's favourite, and we usually pass by it on our walks. It's a small, old Japanese-style house with a thicket of lilies by the front door. They're large white lilies, but the stems and leaves are so overgrown that they almost look like weeds.

"Just a bit," I say. Teaching piano isn't a very lucrative business.

"–," says Soko. "– says you're really pretty. And that you and I look alike."

I have no idea who she's talking about, but for now I say, "Really?" From the way Soko's talking about her friend, I figure I'm supposed to know who she is.

"Which way do you want to go?" asks Soko, standing at a three-way intersection. "If we go that way, we'll see Andy. But if we go that way, we can buy bread."

"The other way," I say, pointing toward the street that leads to the middle school.

"Okay," says Soko, and continues walking.

Andy is a dog that's always chained to a garage with a wisteria trellis. I have no idea how Soko found out its name.

◆　◆　◆

After we get back from our walk, we eat breakfast. Then, Mum leaves for work. Hull is open during the day, too, so Mum is gone all day on the weekends.

This is Mum's schedule:

Monday	Hull is closed. One piano lesson in the morning.
Tuesday	Hull from late afternoon.
Wednesday	Two lessons in the morning. Hull from late afternoon.
Thursday	Hull from late afternoon.
Friday	Hull from late afternoon.
Saturday	Hull all day.
Sunday	Go walking with me in the morning. Hull for the rest of the day.

Mum says she has three new students. She'll probably fit them in on Thursday and Friday mornings. "Work is important," she says. Cigarettes and coffee and chocolate are her sources of nutrients, work is her mood stabilizer, Dad is her rock and the reason she goes on living, and I'm the apple of her eye, her treasure.

She's wearing her polka-dotted skirt today, one of my favourites. It's a navy-blue skirt with white dots. She also has on a white blouse and red lipstick. It might be weird for a daughter to say this about her own mother, but I think Mum's really pretty when she's dressed for work. If only she wouldn't bring anyone like the manager at Tsumiki to our house.

"What is it?" Mum asks, as she looks at me through the mirror.

"Nothing," I say, leaning against the wall. I like watching Mum get ready for work.

I go to Hull for dinner every night. I don't have anything off the regular menu; instead, Mum makes something especially for me. Mum's picky about what I eat, and every month she does a thorough check of my school lunch menu.

In any case, Mum seems satisfied with our new life here – "here, too," to be exact. She never resists new things.

"I'm off," she says with a smile.

"Have a good day." I smile back, still leaning against the wall.

"Avoid peak hours, okay? Sundays are especially busy," Mum says, as she puts her shoes on at the front door. I can't see her feet, but I can tell that she's putting on her dainty strappy sandals. She always wears them with that skirt.

"I know."

"Bye, then," she says once more, and turns around to look at me.

"Have a good day," I say one more time for her sake, and she finally seems resolved to leave and turns the doorknob. The door opens, then shuts behind her.

It's Sunday. I'm left all alone in the "girly flat" that's painted white.

SHORTCUT

The summer is when Hull gets most of its business. In addition to the regulars who go yachting every weekend, the place becomes packed with couples who come for the sun and surf, families on vacation, and student travellers bursting with energy.

There's a piano at Hull, but I don't play. Only rarely, at night, when there are just a few regular customers left and business has been good, does Sachiko, the owner's wife, play the piano. She always wears a checked shirt.

On several occasions, I've been asked to play something, but I've declined every time. Professionals shouldn't play unless they're going to be paid. That's what the Professor taught me. Sachiko and her husband are kind and they've been very good to me, so everyone must think that I'm pretty pig-headed not to play the piano for them at all.

"What are you reading, Soko?" Sachiko asks. It's past ten o'clock, and all the customers are gone. Soko's been reading by herself since she finished dinner.

"Essays by Karel Capek," Soko replies. She's grown so tall since she started middle school and has become a young woman in her own right. Last week she got her hair cut short, so her slender neck is exposed.

"She's going to be a beauty," the Professor said when Soko was born. Soko was just a tiny newborn at the time.

"We don't know that yet," I said.

The Professor, in all seriousness, said, "Beauties are made, not born. Girls don't grow up beautiful on their own, they're raised beautiful."

It was winter, and we were drinking tea in the study. Though the room was small, everything in it was arranged to suit the Professor's tastes.

I'd already decided then that I'd leave the Professor before long, and he knew. We had discussed things over and over, and there was nothing more to talk about. That day, I think he was trying to stop me from leaving.

"If Soko stays here, she's going to be beautiful." That's what he said. "At the very least, I'll provide a life for her where she'll want for nothing."

Want. Sometimes, I think about wanting. Ever since I was a child, I'd wanted to be free. Rather, I had a need for freedom, just like one's need for food and sleep. I fought for freedom. I left home in pursuit of freedom. But freedom and wanting are actually extremely similar, and sometimes I can't tell the difference.

I wonder if Soko is wanting now.

"We have some lime sorbet. Do you want some before you go home?" Sachiko asks, and I shake my head.

"How about you, Soko?" Sachiko asks.

Soko looks at me, so I gesture with my hand as if to say, "Go ahead."

"Yes, please," Soko says.

Although Hull is a restaurant and bar, it closes early. Eleven, at the latest. People who live by the ocean apparently don't stay up late.

My art teacher, Mr Sawada, always wears jeans. He has big, shapely hands, and speaks softly. I imagine Dad's hands to be like his. I don't know why.

I watch Mum as I eat my lime sorbet. She's behind the counter, washing glasses as she jokes with her boss and his wife.

My mum is a bit unusual. She got married right after she graduated from college, but then she met my dad and had "a bone-melting love affair," and had me.

Mum says that she and Dad were "simply the perfect match."

School's out for the summer, and I wait for Mum to get off of work so that we can ride home together on her scooter. It feels so good to ride by the ocean, hanging on to Mum's back. I smell the ocean. Mum says the sky is filled with stars, but I can't see because my helmet is in the way.

Sometimes we stop and walk along the beach. The sound of waves, the lights on the opposite shore, the reddish-purplish seaweed that's been washed up onto the sand. When we walk on the beach at night, Mum always takes her shoes off.

"It's not safe, Mum," I say, and she shrugs, as if there's nothing she can do about it.

"I know. Your dad used to say the same thing."

It's my turn to shrug. Maybe it's because Mum's got good vision, but she's yet to cut herself from walking barefoot.

Even during the summer, I go to school twice a week to swim. The pool is located behind the corridor connecting two school buildings. There are lots of trees growing on the hill right next to our school, so the pool is half covered in shade. It gives it a really luxurious, resort-like feel to it.

"The pool's surrounded by so much vegetation," Mum said. She rides her scooter to piano lessons during the day (she has six students!) and apparently passes by sometimes and takes a peek.

"I can't see you when you're in the water, but if you're by the pool, I can tell which one you are even from far away," she said.

By the poolside, we all sit on the ground hugging our knees, our bodies wet. Our classmates' wet feet patter by in front of us, lots and lots of them. They spray water droplets, pinch their noses, and make smacking sounds as they readjust bathing suits that have gotten wedged into their butts.

On this sunny day there's a breeze, and the leafy shadows of the trees flutter on the surface of the wet, black concrete.

I like this school a lot. I like the small, white, older building and the blue-gray window frames.

When we get home I take a bath, and start reading my book where I left off. The book is a collection of essays with illustrations here and there. It's really good.

"Still up?" Mum says, coming out of the bathroom. "You're such a bookworm."

Mum's always reading, too, though.

She chuckles. "I guess it's to be expected. You came into existence when your dad and I were both reading."

A long, long time ago, at a cottage resort on some Mediterranean island, I came into existence as a result of "absolute inevitability," to use Mum's words. A result of a thick mystery novel, a cocktail called a Sicilian Kiss, and lips that were sigh-inducing.

"When the new semester begins…" I say, as I slide into my futon. We sleep side-by-side on two futon mattresses. "When the new semester begins, I think I'm going to join the art club."

Mum looks at my face and says, "Sounds good." She smiles. "You've always liked to draw."

Mum smells like vanilla when she comes out of the bath. We lie next to each other on our backs and stare at the ceiling as we talk.

"I think that's a really good idea."

It's a quiet night. I can hear the groan of the refrigerator.

The great thing about moving to Zushi is the ocean and the availability of fresh vegetables. There's an agricultural co-op stand near the train station where we can get incredibly fresh vegetables. Prickly, bright green hydroponically-grown cucumbers and carrots with the bushy tops still intact. Plump and shiny eggplants and tomatoes.

There's an abundance of fish, too, and it's inexpensive. Today, I bought some golden threadfin bream that was a pretty pink colour.

Sometimes I think about my true love. For example, when I'm on the footbridge. There's a railroad crossing near the station with four tracks running through it. There's a footbridge above the tracks, which is where I often stand, gazing at the people and trains passing below.

I wonder where he is now. Where he is, and what he's doing. Every time I move to a new city, I stop by all the music shops. I browse through magazines like *Player*, *Guitar Magazine*, and *Jazz Life*, but I've never found any messages from him.

When the new semester began, I joined the art club just like I'd planned. We meet twice a week. Right now, we're doing sketches.

Yoriko, the girl I'm closest to in my class, is in the gymnastics club. We usually walk home together on days our clubs don't meet.

Mum seems busy with piano lessons lately. It's because her students are giving their first recital in the spring, and some of them are taking several lessons a week. Mum's playing a lot of piano these days, too. After spending a couple of hours warming up her fingers with Hanon and Bach, she moves on to Fauré and Schubert. Fauré's and Schubert's pieces are beautiful. But beautiful pieces are sort of melancholy.

"If you ever feel like running away from home…" Mum suddenly said the other day. It was a Sunday, and we were on our weekly morning walk. "If you ever feel like running away from home, you can." Mum supposedly ran away lots of times when she was a kid. "Just make sure to let me know once in a while that you're okay."

I told her I understood. But I'll probably never run away. I know this about myself. Mum seemed to feel better when I told her I understood.

It's October. When the air clears, and the sky turns blue.

"Good morning," Mum says sleepily, having just woken up. I'm preparing breakfast. She puts a cigarette in her mouth and lights it. Her eyes still heavy, Mum sets up the espresso maker and switches it on.

"I dreamt about him," she says. She sometimes dreams about Dad.

"What was it like?" I ask, even though I know the answer. I pour milk over the cereal in my bowl.

"I forgot. But it was a good dream."

Mum never tells me about her dreams. She always says she's forgotten. I don't know whether she really forgets, or whether she remembers but doesn't want to tell me. Either way, it's the same. For Mum, dreams about Dad are always good dreams. No matter what.

"Nice weather," Mum says, looking out the window. Mum looks pale in the mornings.

I'm a little jealous of her. I had dreams about Dad a few times when I was little, but they were all vague and blurry, and I haven't dreamt about him since. Mum's able to dream about him because she remembers him. At least she sees him in her sleep.

The espresso maker gurgles. I take a bite of my egg, sunny-side-up, sprinkled with salt.

✦ ✦ ✦

In the dream, he was smiling. An unbelievably beautiful smile. I've never seen a smile as beautiful as his.

What beautiful eyes, I thought as I dreamt.

What a beautiful forehead. That's what I thought next.

We were somewhere quiet, somewhere outdoors. The sun shone on one side of his face.

I've got to go.

I knew that was what he was thinking. He knew that I knew. There was a hint of sadness in his eyes. I was sad, too. Neither of us said so, but we knew this was the last time we'd see each other.

"What's that package?" Soko, who's been eating breakfast across from me at the table, asks.

"Hmm?"

An egg, sunny-side-up, cereal, tea, and Soko in her school uniform. A scene from my real life.

"Oh, it's lipstick," I answer, as I stand up and pour coffee into a teacup. "There are eight in there. New colors, apparently. Mrs Ikuta gave them to me."

Mrs Ikuta is one of my piano students, whose husband works for a cosmetics company.

"If you see any you like, you can have them. I don't really think I'll use any of them."

Soko looks uninterested but says, "Uh-huh."

"Mrs Ikuta's piano is a white Young Chang. She says it used to belong to her husband's mother." I sip my coffee and light my second cigarette. "Her daughter used to play the piano, but she's studying in Canada right now."

"Huh," Soko says, and finishes her tea. "Are they rich?"

"Probably."

They live in a big house. There's an oil painting hanging by the front door, and the piano room is soundproof.

"It's weird," says Soko. "You don't resist new things. But you never grow accustomed to them, either."

I cock my head. The Professor once said the same thing to me.

"You don't ever settle into a place. You don't stand out, but you don't blend in, either."

According to the Professor, it wasn't necessarily a bad thing that I don't, but makes those around me feel very alone.

"Bye, Mum. I'm off." Soko gets up, and without explaining what it is she thinks I don't resist or grow accustomed to, goes to the bathroom to wash her face and hands.

It's late afternoon, and I'm wiping the windows at Hull when Sachiko approaches me and says, "Maybe I'll cut my hair, too." She has long hair, which she always keeps loosely pulled back.

"You and Soko have inspired me to cut my hair short."

I don't know how to respond, so I just smile meekly.

"Soko looks good with short hair, doesn't she? Though at first, I thought it was a shame that she got rid of it all."

Boss and Sachiko don't have any children.

"I think long hair is nice, too," I say, because I don't know what else to say. Elaborate models of yachts adorn the bay windows at Hull. Elaborate models and small pumpkins.

"You've been travelling a lot, right?" Sachiko says. "Soko told me. That you two are birds of passage."

The air outside is a light blue, and the dry, faded leaves on the trees – they have yet to completely change colour – flutter in the wind.

"Short hair seems so liberating," Sachiko says, and again, I smile weakly.

I close the lid of the window cleanser, place the bottle and the cloth I've been using in a basket, and put everything back in the closet. The sky has darkened, and streetlamps begin to light up and reflect against the windows I've just cleaned. There's a faint lemony scent lingering from the cleanser. Suddenly, I'm unbearably lonely.

"I'll be right back," I tell Sachiko, and go on a walk for about ten minutes. I walk forcefully, with big steps. There's a chill in the air.

This is not a world where he doesn't exist, I think to myself as I walk.

This is a world that follows my encounter with him. So everything's okay. Everything is fine.

The way I mark time is practically like BC and AD in the Gregorian calendar. Come to think of it, he probably is my God.

"I swear, I will find you again, Yoko."

That's what he said.

I smoke a cigarette and hum a Rod Stewart song. When I close my eyes, it feels like my true love is holding me in his arms.

SPRING HAS COME

The straw festoons at Hisagi Shrine are a pale salmon pink, as though they've been dyed with safflower. After passing through the *torii* and reaching the top of the stone steps, there's a statue of the god Inari visible toward the back of the shrine grounds and red cloth banners lining the path leading to it. With both hands in the pockets of my coat, I wander around. During the day, there's absolutely no one else here.

Way back when, my true love and I used to take a lot of walks. We went all over the place. We both liked walking and never grew the least bit tired. We could keep going forever. Always holding hands.

My true love and I walked to every corner of the city where I was living with the Professor. It didn't matter where we were, as long as we were together. And plus, there was really nowhere for us to go.

"I'm sorry we're always walking," he often said. I, of course, shook my head, but no words came to me. We both probably knew that if we stopped walking, we'd have no choice but to go home, separately.

As I walk down the shrine's stone steps, I think about him. His face after two days without shaving, the gentleness of his voice when he sang to me, the slight furrowing of his eyebrows when he smoked a cigarette, how surprisingly warm his body was when our legs became entangled in bed.

The serious look in his eyes when he said, "We'll always be together."

Then I think about Soko, who now wears a uniform – a white blouse, a navy blue vest, and a pleated navy blue skirt – to school every day.

Our Soko, who now says things like, "I think you should learn to be more realistic, Mum." At some point, she'd packed away her doll Allie and her pink bear somewhere in her closet.

Someday, when we meet again and I tell him about Soko, I wonder what he'll say.

The January wind has a gentle dryness to it and smells of a peaceful residential neighbourhood. Not far from the shrine is Soko's school.

✦ ✦ ✦

When I get home from school, Mum's at a piano lesson. Hull's been closed since Christmas, so Mum's been putting a lot of effort into teaching piano. Every year Hull stays closed for the winter because the owner and his wife go yachting somewhere for a long time. Mum told me that they're in Menton this year. They have a lot of money.

"The money we make at Hull isn't enough to even cover mooring fees," the owner once said, laughing. But he runs some company and owns a block of flats somewhere. Different people have such different lives.

In Mum's words, our life is a rock that keeps rolling until we meet Dad again. Mum chose this life years ago.

"I chose to live it," Mum once said, emphasizing the "I." I was sitting on her lap, and she was stroking my hair.

"So if we never see your dad and we end up just rolling around like a rock, he's not to blame."

That might be true. But, well, Mum's the one who made the choice, not me.

"Does Dad break promises?" I asked. At the time, I was still little and was unsettled by her suggestion.

"Promises?"

"Isn't Dad supposed to come find us, wherever we are? Didn't he promise?"

"Oh, right," Mum said, and smiled tenderly. "Of course Dad doesn't break promises." She then kissed the top of my head and said, "Dad's promise was fulfilled as soon as it was uttered."

I like the month of January, because that's when the third trimester begins, and I've gotten used to things at school by then. I turn on the radio as I look at the calendar in the kitchen, then drink some milk, quickly get my homework out of the way, and pick up where I left off on the art club project that I have to hand in tomorrow. Alone by myself in the room, without Mum.

For the project, I have to divide a sheet of paper in half and draw the same motif from different angles on each half. I've chosen to draw a house by the ocean. It's a light blue house by the beach that I see in the distance on my walks. Mum told me that it's a restaurant. In the evening when the lights are on, it looks like a mansion in some fairytale from a foreign country. I like it a lot.

I finished sketching it yesterday, and today I add colour to it. I like to paint, but I don't like the nose-tickling smell of watercolors. Actually, there are a lot of smells I'm not too excited about. The smell on buses and trains. Beauty parlours. The school lunch kitchen. The gym equipment room. Dried up fish and seaweed on the beach.

"You're overly sensitive to smells," Mum says. "Yes, everything has a smell, but I think each smell is unique and interesting."

Mum only looks on the bright side of things.

Incidentally, Dad's skin smells like sunlight, according to Mum. And depending on the day, it might have the scent of gin, a blanket, the leaves of a linden tree, or salt mixed in. I have no idea what that would smell like.

I learned about what Dad smells like just last month on his forty-third birthday. As usual, Mum and I sang "Happy Birthday," ate cake, used the self-timer on the camera to take a picture of ourselves, and talked about Dad.

"His hair smelled like autumn."

"Autumn?"

My Mum's a romantic.

This year, Mum made Queen of Nata. I have no idea who this queen is, but the cake's been one of Mum's specialities for a long time. It's a crumbly, egg-coloured sponge cake with lots of whipped cream.

"I wonder who Dad's spending his birthday with," I said.

Mum thought about it for a while and smiled ruefully. Then she said, "Who knows?"

After we had some cake, Mum played the piano. Some of the pieces I knew, and some I didn't. That night, Mum played the piano by herself for a really long time.

✦ ✦ ✦

After work, I return home after picking up some things I need for dinner. It's a particularly cold evening, and there are already stars in the dusky blue sky. Soko is painting.

"Hey, you're back," Soko says.

"Yep," I say, and lightly hug Soko from behind. "Did you have a good day?"

"Stop, you're going to make me spill the water," Soko says, with the paintbrush in her hand. Still, she dutifully continues, "Yeah, I had a good day. We had both English reading and grammar."

Soko likes English.

"*Spring has come*," I say – an English sentence I learned long ago – but Soko, appearing confused, merely shrugs.

After dinner, I read as I soak my feet in a pail of hot water. It's a mystery novel about a lone-wolf detective. The room is warm and smells of gas from the gas heater.

Winter is when all living things sleep.

That's what the Professor used to say. He was sensitive to the cold, and always got sick at the beginning of winter, but he still preferred winter to summer. He said the reason was because wisdom and civilization were required in the wintertime.

I didn't care about the seasons then. All seasons pass, and they all return. I figured they were merely external changes in our environment. At least that's what I thought until I met my true love.

I put a cigarette in my mouth and light up. It's a quiet night. Soko is already asleep in the next room.

Spring came and with it the new school year, and I started eighth grade in one piece. The recital Mum's students gave at a small rented auditorium was pretty well received, and now she has another new student. Mum and I went to a hot springs during spring break. The crocuses that we're growing in our classroom bloomed. Mum's boss and his wife came back with tans, and they've been back in business for the past couple of weeks.

But I'm feeling a bit depressed. It's only been a year since we came to Zushi, but Mum already seems to be considering another move.

I realized this when we went to the hot spring, and Mum asked our server if they were hiring. Of course, it's possible she may not have been serious about it when she asked. Mum does a lot of things like that. She'll say, "Let's live in France," or "I wonder what the process of immigrating to Hong Kong entails," with an earnestness that hardly seems like she's joking. And every time, I'm a bit taken aback. Because knowing her, it's quite possible she might follow through.

In any case, some day this year or next, or the year after that, Mum will say to me, "I'm thinking we should move. What do you think?"

It depresses me to think about it. Even when I'm sitting in the art room on a sunny day like today.

The art room is my favourite place in school. The time I spend at the art club is when I'm happiest.

There are almost thirty art club members, but only about half show up on a regular basis. I have no idea why the others don't come.

Just because it's the art club, it doesn't mean we're always drawing. Yeah, we sketch in our sketchbooks for the first twenty minutes every time we meet, but after that, we do different kinds of activities. If there aren't that many people, like today, we look at art books or watch videos. On more rare occasions, Mr Sawada, our adviser, serves us coffee. Not the kind you get from vending machines, but real fresh coffee that he makes in his office. I never drink coffee out of the can, because like Mum says, they put a "murderous amount of sugar" in them.

"That's Pierre Bonnard," Mr Sawada says, his eyes on the page I'm staring at. His voice is quiet and gentle.

"Bust in profile, red background," I read the caption on the painting out loud. It's a beautiful painting. The woman in it looks like Mum.

When I was much younger, I liked moving. I looked forward to new places, as long as I was with Mum.

But just because I liked something when I was little, I don't think it means I have to keep liking it.

"Should we wrap up for today?" Mr Sawada says, and we put away the art books and photo collections. Today, he's wearing a beige shirt and a moss green jacket.

✦ ✦ ✦

With the arrival of spring, there's a surge in the number of ships leaving the harbour. You learn a lot just looking out at the ocean from the window of the restaurant. Like the fact that the colour of the water depends not on the seasons but on the weather, or that the names of ships are written from left to right on one side but are written backwards, from right to left on the other, or that Frisbees seem to be popular among young people again.

Spring here smells like water.

"Yoko." It's Mr Wakatsuki, the third-generation owner of a well-established Japanese confectionery store, and a regular customer at Hull.

"Yes?"

"Could I have another espresso?"

He often comes here for lunch. He says he wants to stare at the ocean at least during lunch.

"Oh, over here, too," says Mr Kono, who works at the market.

"Sure," I say with a smile, and exchange their ashtrays with fresh ones.

During spring break, Soko and I went to a hot springs in Hakone. We took a cute little train running through the mountains. It was a fun trip. We had relaxing meals in our room. It'd been the first time we did anything like that. We both bathed until our cheeks were nice and shiny, then slipped on our *yukata*. I had a little bit of sake; Soko also had a sip from a tiny cup. As soon as it touched her lips, she winced. "It smells like sake," she said.

I laughed. "What an unoriginal thing to say."

She's *our* daughter. There's no way she won't enjoy drinking.

In the middle of the night, we took another dip in the outdoor bath with a roof overhead. There were stars. I watched Soko from behind, her legs long, so free and straight. This was our Soko, both mine and his.

Neither Mr Wakatsuki nor Mr Kono stays for long because they have to get back to work. Tourists don't stay long, either, because they've got sights to see. On weekdays, there's a high turnover during the day.

In the afternoon, when business is slow, I work on the weeds that are growing around the restaurant. I like weeding. Right now, yellow roses are in bloom behind the restaurant.

Soko arrives in the evening.

"Hello," she says every day as she comes in through the back door. She reads or does her homework at a corner table.

Her dinner tonight consists of salmon, steamed vegetables, and rice. Soko always eats whatever I make without leaving a crumb.

"How was your day?"

Soko, who's wearing a grey and white striped t-shirt, jeans, and grey trainers, is sitting on a chair with her legs stretched out.

"So-so," she says. "How was yours, Mum?"

"So-so," I also say. It's our routine back-and-forth.

"How was the art club?"

"We sketched and worked on wax sculptures."

"How's your adviser?"

"Fine, I guess."

Soko seems to have a crush on her art teacher. According to her, the teacher is "very tactful." And "A 'teacher with tact' is practically an oxymoron."

In any case, I have mixed feelings about it. About both mother and daughter having the hots for their teachers.

Some days, Soko stays until closing time and goes home with me on the back of my scooter, and others days she takes the bus home early. Today, she says she'll go ahead without me.

"Be safe," I say from behind the counter.

"Okay," Soko says. "Mum, I have to talk to you about something tonight. I'll wait up, so don't be too late, okay?"

"What is it?" I ask.

Soko shakes her head and says, "I'll tell you when you get home." I'm suddenly nervous.

"Yoko, can I have a beer?" a customer hollers, so I signal to Soko with a wave to get going.

As a little girl, every time I unlocked the door of an empty house, my imagination went wild. I envisioned that ghosts and bugs and monsters hiding inside would come flying out as soon as I opened the door. But I was only ever scared for a moment. In my mind, these bad creatures were never violent. All they did was escape. So I would let them out, and go inside. That's when I'd run into the loser that didn't make it out.

In the image I had in my head, the loser is purple and looks like a small doll. Its face is ashen and sinister-looking, but it would be terrified because it's still a little monster. Eventually, we'd become friends.

I don't have wild ideas like that anymore. I just unlock the door and go in. There are photos and a figurine of an angel decorating the entrance.

Mum comes home early, bearing chocolates that she says were a gift from a customer.

"Is it okay if I shower first?" she asks, as she takes off her coat and scarf. Sure, I say.

"I'll be right back. And leave the chocolates for tomorrow, okay?"

Mum always has a grand air about her when she comes home from work. It's as if you can almost smell the outside world on her.

"I will," I say, accept a hug from Mum – still a ritual between us when she comes home – and continue reading.

We sit at the kitchen table across from each other in the middle of the night, drinking coffee. Having just come out of the shower, Mum's skin has a bit of a glossy shine to it. Mum regularly coats her face with lots of moisturiser during the winter because her skin gets dry.

"So, what did you want to talk about?" she asks, and takes a sip of her coffee.

"About moving," I answer.

"Moving?"

"Yeah. I don't want to move until I finish middle school."

Mum's expression remains unchanged. She takes a good look at me, gives a small shrug, and says, "Fine." Cool as a cucumber.

"That's it?"

"Yeah." How anticlimactic. "You know, because I've gotten used to things here," I add, even though Mum hasn't asked me why I don't want to move.

"Is it important to get used to things?" Mum asks, and lights a cigarette.

"For me, it is." Mum probably doesn't feel the need to adapt. "I want to be settled in." I try to explain that it's not the moving itself I hate, but rather the possibility that we may move at anytime, and that the possibility stops me from feeling comfortable anywhere. That I hate being in constant fear. Like the loser who's left behind by all the other monsters who escape the empty house.

"You might not understand, Mum, but I want to live someplace I know well. I want to live in a place I'm accustomed to, surrounded by people I know."

Mum doesn't say anything. For a while, we drink our coffee in silence.

"I'm going to bed, okay?" I say, feeling sort of sad. I get up and take my cup to the sink.

"Soko."

"Yeah?" I turn on the faucet and wash my cup.

"I know I've asked a lot of you," Mum says quietly. "I know it would be really nice if we could live in a familiar place among familiar people."

"Then why don't we—"

"It's impossible," Mum says, stopping me in mid-sentence. "Because I've settled into him. I can't grow accustomed to anything else."

"You're just not trying, right?"

"That's not it," Mum says. She looks straight into my eyes. "That's not it," she says calmly.

Maybe it's true. Maybe Mum can't get used to anything or anybody but Dad.

"In any case…" I say, utterly miserable now. "In any case, I just don't want to move yet."

I can't look at Mum.

I never thought that hearing the words, "Fine, I understand," would be so heartbreaking.

THE HIGHWAY

When my Mum and Dad lived by the ocean, they had a big dog. Mum says they could see the ocean from their bedroom window. They rose early when they lived there, and would take the dog out for a walk by the ocean. Apparently, Mum was always struck by glimpses of Dad's ankles below the hems of his trousers, which he rolled up when they went barefoot on the beach.

They would then go home and eat, and spend the morning reading.

They swam a lot in the summer, of course. Mum can't swim, but apparently she could swim forever if she clung to Dad's back. Not that that can really be called swimming.

Mum says that as long as Dad was with her, no waves could ever frighten her. She says it didn't matter how deep the water was.

The story of when Mum and Dad used to live by the ocean is a fairytale that Mum's been telling me since I was little.

It's my second summer in Zushi.

This morning, Mum and I go for a walk. Our Sunday morning walk. After filling our lungs with the ocean breeze on the beach, we walk through streets lined with houses back to our apartment. During our walks, Mum will sit anywhere without a second thought, so the hem and back of her long flared skirt get dirty.

We run into the lady from the greengrocer's in front of the post office. It's the lady she buys our vegetables from all the time, but Mum doesn't recognize her.

"Good morning. It's hot, isn't it?" Mum says, smiling, but asks me who that was after she's gone. Mum doesn't remember people. She doesn't get used to places or people.

"I'm surprised you actually get by as a waitress," I say, and Mum shrugs.

"Work is a completely different matter."

The day before yesterday, Yoriko and I stopped by Zushi station on our way home from school. It was sunny and hot out. After a snack at McDonald's (without telling Mum, since I'm not allowed to eat fast food), we browsed books at the bookstore.

"Soko, do you sometimes see your dad?" Yoriko suddenly asked. It's too complicated to explain, so I tell everyone at school that my parents are divorced.

"No," I said, putting down a fashion magazine. I picked up a mail-order fashion catalogue and flipped through.

"Never?"

"Nope," I said. It was true, so I didn't feel guilty saying it.

"What about child support and stuff?"

I told her I really didn't know much about the whole thing.

The area surrounding Zushi station was bright and humming with activity. The black tiles of a mosaic embedded in the concrete ground shone in the sun.

It's Sunday. I draw all afternoon, all alone in a white, girly apartment. In the kitchen, Mum has left me lunch she made (though I haven't eaten it yet), and there's mindless babble and pop music coming from the radio. Mum doesn't like air-conditioning and rarely turns it on. During the day when she's not here, though, I keep it on constantly.

✦ ✦ ✦

Summer is a special time.

Every one of my cells has preserved its memories. And summer is when each one of them is suddenly awakened, trembling restlessly.

It's Sunday. The lunchtime customers have thinned out, and I'm in my thoughts as I wipe the countertop. The air outside the window shimmers in the heat.

"Someone gave me two tickets to a ballgame. Would you be interested in going?" my boss asks, and I shake my head.

"Why don't you go with Sachiko?"

Sachiko, who is watering the potted plants, says that baseball is boring and doesn't want to go.

"I have to focus on work during the summer," he says, and smiles wryly.

Soko says she's going on an overnight school trip next month. It's a trip that includes volunteer activities and Zen meditation. To each her own summer.

It was during the summer that I met my true love. And it was also during the summer that he went away.

Two years! All of that happened in just two years. Everything that ever changed my life, everything that eventually set Soko's life in motion happened in that time.

Every one of my cells was formed in those two years.

"Yoko, do you want some coffee?" Sachiko asks.

Yes, I say, and open the cabinet. Me too, says her husband, and I line up three mugs on the counter.

Today was the last day of the semester. I did well on my final exams. I pop into Hull in the afternoon, and then walk alone along the highway. The road has relatively little traffic. Mum and I come here a lot together. Grass has sprung from both sides of the road, and I yank out tall blades as I walk. Mum, who's a scaredy-cat, doesn't like to go through the tunnel with the sidewalk that Mum and I call "the dark forest." But it doesn't scare me at all. It's short, so if you stand on one end you can see the other end, bright and dome-shaped. It's a dusty tunnel.

School's out for the summer.

At night, Mum and I chat a little bit as we drink coffee. The topic of our conversation is Mr Sawada.

"Be wary of words," Mum says, as she sews on a button that's fallen off the blouse of my school uniform. "Teachers are generally very clever with their words."

Mum says words are dangerous. According to her, you're a goner if you feel someone's touched you with his words, if he's touched you in a place in your heart that you've never been touched before. I don't totally get what she's talking about. But I do know that Mr Sawada's words touch my heart with ease. And that he has a really nice voice. I got an A in art again this semester. Just as I'd expected.

"All done," Mum says, and I put the blouse Mum hands me in the laundry basket.

"Was the Professor good with his words, too?" I ask.

"Oh, was he ever," Mum says. "My heart soaked up his words like they were rain."

Like rain.

"Because I was so lonely," Mum adds, smiling. When Mum talks about the Professor, she gets a gentle look on her face. A gentle, nostalgic look.

"What about Dad?" I ask.

Mum raises her eyebrows, as if my question had come out of the blue. She thinks about it for a little bit and says, "We didn't need words." She slowly lights a cigarette and adds, "Words were completely useless to us."

Mum is staring at the wall. She's here, but it's like she's not. Mum gets that way sometimes when she talks about Dad. My mum. People say we look like sisters.

"Hmm."

We take turns taking a bath, slather on Mum's body lotion from the round, light pink bottle, say good night, and go to sleep.

✦ ✦ ✦

August flies by frantically. There are my shifts at Hull, piano lessons, Soko's overnight trip, and her swimming classes.

Our screen window breaks and we have to call a repairman to get it fixed.

"It would be so nice to have a man around the house at times like this," Soko says so cheekily it makes me laugh. And then I teach her the truth.

"Not all men can fix screens, you know."

The Professor wasn't good at things like that. Like opening tight jar lids, carrying heavy things, and crushing used moving boxes.

"Don't think you can rely on men for everything," I say, and Soko grows sullen.

"You're not one to talk, Mum."

She's right, so I laughed. She really has a point.

The days go by without a hitch, and yet I go on waiting for him.

"I'll be back," he'd said. "Believe me. Don't doubt me for a second. I swear, I'll find you, Yoko, no matter where you are. I have to go away for a short while, but I'm with you in spirit no matter where I am. I'll be back. Soon."

Soon.

It was September. It was a hot and humid evening, and the park near his shop was filled with a thick green scent.

It's been a while since that day.

In the fall, Soko's still life painting wins second place in the city art fair.

"I'll bet you're going to become a master painter," I say, but Soko dismisses the possibility outright. She apparently wants to become a simultaneous interpreter or a veterinarian when she grows up.

"You're looking at that painting again," Mr Sawada says. It's our fifteen-minute break between second and third period. "You like that book, don't you?"

I nod. "It's so beautiful."

Now he nods.

"The paintings are by an artist who painted a lot of nudes and still lifes about a hundred years ago. His landscapes haven't left much of an impression on me, though he's painted quite a few of them."

Today Mr Sawada is wearing a brown turtleneck and jeans.

"But you can see a bit of landscape outside the windows and doors in this one," I say, and he laughs. The bell rings just then, so I reluctantly close the book.

"That painting."

"Yes?"

He takes the book and opens the page to a painting called "The Table."

"The girl in this painting kind of looks like you."

It's a painting of a big white table. There's a girl sitting on the far end of it. I'm on cloud nine.

After school, Yoriko and I stop by McDonald's on our way home.

"Mr Sawada?" Yoriko says rather indifferently, as she pulls the straw in her Coke away from her mouth. "Isn't he kind of wimpy-looking?"

Yoriko is glum, probably because of our achievement test results. She doesn't do too well in school. The achievement test we take in the fall of eighth grade can affect our choice of high schools.

I see a bus go by outside the window. It's a strange bus that I see sometimes, a bus bound for Kamakura, with a painting on its side. Every time I see it I think about running away, only because the bus is kind of mysterious. Mum says she ran away lots of times when she was in middle school, alone. Because she didn't know what else to do.

"Hey," Yoriko says as she shoves a long, thin French fry into her mouth. "Do you think your mum will ever get remarried?"

"No," I respond, and finish the rest of my Coke. The ice rattles around in the paper cup, which has become soft and flimsy.

"Hmm. But she's so pretty. She probably just has bad luck with men."

"Bad luck!"

I tell Mum what Yoriko said when she gets home at night, and she puts on an exaggerated expression.

"No one else has as much good luck with men as I do," she says, adds that Yoriko has no idea what she's talking about, and shrugs. I refrain from making any comments.

"Here's some chocolate," Mum says, and puts today's bounty on the table. They're from Neuhaus.

✦ ✦ ✦

In November, I experience the biggest crisis of my life. Soko tells me she wants to live in a dorm.

Am I going to lose her? It can't be.

I ponder this question as I walk blindly along the beach. It's a cloudy, windy day.

Soko, going far away? How can it be? She's only in middle school. Little Soko. My third gift, with a spine just like his.

There's no one at the beach. The sand that's been swept ashore by the waves has dried a hushed grey, and small branches and plastic bags lie about looking forlorn.

"I've decided where I want to go to high school," Soko said nonchalantly last night. "I was told I can get a recommendation. Though who knows if I'll get in."

"What do you mean, 'who knows?' You get such great grades."

"Well, it's a really competitive school," Soko laughed, embarrassed.

"No dorms. No way," I said, but Soko was unfazed.

"I'll come home on the weekends. It's not like I'm going to a foreign country. Visits are allowed at the dorm, and you can also come see me at school, so it won't be that much different from the way things are now."

I was stunned.

"What do you mean, 'visits are allowed'? It's not a prison. Give me a break."

Really, give me a break. I have to stop this from happening. There must be something I can do.

Apparently, the school is also in Kanagawa prefecture, where we live right now. It's in some city called Kurihira, which, according to Soko, is "just a stone's throw away" from Zushi.

"Look."

The school pamphlet Soko handed me includes a graph indicating the school's ranking, a list of what its graduates have gone on to do, the number of applicants from the previous year, and tuition, in addition to photographs of students wearing their school uniforms and of the school's facilities.

"The students go to China for their graduation trip," Soko continued.

"China? You want to go to China? Is that what this is about?" I asked, and Soko sighed with a look of disgust. "Why do you have to live in a dorm? Why can't you just commute from home? We won't move for the three years you're in high school. I promise. Wait, let's move to Kurihira."

The more I spoke, the sadder Soko looked.

"I've already made my decision."

Soko's small face with her chubby cheeks betrayed her determination.

"But why?" I asked, unconvinced. It's always been the two of us. We've stayed here for the three years Soko's been in middle school, just like she wanted.

"Just because. I've already decided."

Soko was being stubborn.

"This is reality," she said, without looking at me. "I want to live in the real world. You're not facing the real world."

I had no idea what she was talking about. I just stared blankly at Soko, whose face had become twisted amid her tears.

"I'm sorry," Soko said, in agony.

"What are you apologizing for?"

Soko was bawling. She cried uncontrollably, blew her nose in an attempt to stop, then started sobbing again. Then, sombrely she said, "For not being able to stay in your world forever."

It's blustery out.

The wind creates ripples on the surface of the dull, still ocean.

I felt I shouldn't cry. I shouldn't. If I did, it'd mean that I'd accepted Soko's decision. The "reality" that Soko referred to. Though that's not what it's like at all. It's not.

But I didn't know what to do. That's why I'm walking blindly, like a crazy woman. Like a crazy woman who's been rejected by reality.

My black ankle boots are sticky from the sand and salt. So is my hair, skin, coat, and skirt.

I wish he were here. If only he were here, he'd stop Soko.

"No."

That's what I kept saying last night.

"I'm not letting you live in a dorm, and I won't pay your tuition, either. I won't look at any paperwork, and I won't go to the parents' interview."

Soko didn't object. She looked at me with utter exhaustion, like an abandoned dog.

The streetlamps are beginning to light up. I climb up the embankment and walk along the highway. A truck drives by loudly. I put a cigarette in my mouth as I continue onward, and finally get it going after several failed attempts to light it. I inhale deeply and exhale. Leaning against the entrance of the tunnel, I slowly smoke the cigarette. It's the tunnel Soko and I call "the dark forest."

It's evening. I have to get back to Hull. No matter how hard I squint, I don't see anything hull-down.

RABBIT EARS

It gets cold in the winter even in Zushi. We got a light dusting of snow last night. It's February now, and aside from the fact that Soko talks less than she used to, our lives haven't changed, and there's been no talk of dormitories since that one time.

But I know. Soko will leave. Just like I ran away from home. But she'll do it with much more poise, and far more prudently than I did.

"Yoko, you're a good girl," my father often said as he sat me on his lap. "You're the best in all the world."

In spite of my being a big troublemaker.

The ocean is a muddy colour, its waves heavy. It's a deserted winter ocean. Recently my walks have merely become routine. I don't enjoy them; they sort of make me feel hopeless. Even though I still get the feeling that my true love might come walking in my direction.

I walk on the beach listening to Rod Stewart, and stare at the grey sky. Hope is not something that exists in the future, but something that's here in the present.

The song 'Have I Told You Lately' starts playing, and suddenly I'm about to cry. The Rod Stewart CD was a gift from him a long time ago. A really long time ago.

Soko had some harsh words for me last week. I don't want to keep reminding myself of the incident, but then again, I can't forget. Of course I can't blame her. She's never met him.

I pick up a piece of wood and carry it in my hand without purpose as I walk. It's a habit. Whenever I walk on the beach I pick things up. Soko has a tendency to do the same meaningless thing. When we take walks together, sooner or later we find our hands full.

I look toward the sky, close my eyes, and breathe in the smell of the sea. Today, I teach three lessons. I raised my rates this year, but since my students are all well off, it probably doesn't bother them so much that my monthly fee went from 10,000 yen to 12,000.

✦ ✦ ✦

When I get home, Mum is away at a lesson. On days when I know Mum will be out teaching, I feel less stressed about going home.

Postcards had arrived from the owner of Hull and his wife, who closed up their restaurant to go abroad like they do every year. One each for Mum and me. They're supportive of my choice of high schools.

On the table, there's a note from Mum and a snack. I change out of my uniform and fold the laundry, eat my snack, and start studying. The school I want to go to is a tough one to get into. Enough for me to want to ask for some backup from Dad's genes. Mum says he's incredibly intelligent.

But I have a more realistic vision of what one can and can't count on than Mum does. That's why I'm studying hard. Plus, I like studying. Even if I'm just studying for a test.

Still, I'm mentally preparing myself for the possibility that I might not get in on the first try. The school allows students who aren't accepted on their first attempt to re-apply the following year. If Mum doesn't change her mind, I'll have to save money. In that case, I'm planning to work next year while I study to take the exams again. Mum's boss says that he'd be willing to hire me if it comes to that.

"Taking an extra year to apply to high school is a waste of time," he told Mum in my support. "If it's about the money, we'll do whatever we can to help you out. And if Soko is adamant about paying us back, then she can take all the time she needs to do it."

Mum was so upset that she could barely speak.

"This is none of your business," she said, when she finally found her voice.

If Sachiko-san hadn't intervened, I think Mum would've quit Hull right then and there. But Mum should be angry with me, not them. I used to think that Mum was a lot more rational when it came to things like that.

Some things you can count on and others things you can't, it turns out.

It's so sad to think about. Mum and I are actually nothing alike.

I hear a noise from the front door and Mum says, "I'm back." Then there's the rustling of a plastic bag.

"Hi," I say, and awkwardly receive Mum's embrace. "It's cold out, isn't it?"

Having come home on her scooter, Mum's cheek is as cold as ice.

"Were you studying again?" Mum says, glancing at the opened books and notebooks on the table.

"Yeah, a little bit," I reply, and despair that I may have hurt Mum's feelings. I know Mum is much happier when I'm painting, eating a snack, reading a book, or clumsily playing the piano. Like I used to when I was little.

"You'll ruin your eyes if you study too much," Mum says as she puts away the groceries.

Can't you at least come up with a better reason I shouldn't study? I spitefully strike back at her in my head.

Recently, Mum's been playing the piano for hours after dinner. They're all songs that I don't know, but she plays one of them so much that I've memorized the melody now. It's a light, gentle, quiet piece. Mum's face is so honest and strong and beautiful when she's playing the piano.

Last week, Mum turned forty-one. I gave her a picture frame and chocolate as a birthday gift. Of course, the chocolates were Mum's favorite: Lindt's chocolates in the red packaging.

"Lots of people give me chocolate," Mum said happily, "but you're the only one who gives me these."

She then hugged me and said, "What a beautiful spine."

I'm sure I looked annoyed. "Don't say that," I said, impulsively. Even though it was Mum's birthday.

"Why not?"

Mum looked surprised. I was suddenly tongue-tied, but eventually said, "Forget it." Mum didn't push the matter any further.

When Mum compliments my spine, I feel like she's actually complimenting Dad, not me. I feel like she's holding me in her arms as Dad's substitute.

"Stop telling me to forget it," Mum said. "I'd been meaning to tell you. I don't like it."

I was infuriated. Because that wasn't what we were talking about. I didn't respond.

"Do you understand?" Mum pressed, which kept me even more closed up. "Soko."

"I'm not Dad. I may have a spine that looks like Dad's, but it isn't his, it's mine."

Mum didn't seem to get it. With a look of a surprise, she said, "Of course it's yours."

"Dad's not here. Do you realize that?"

As soon as the words were out of mouth, I regretted saying them. I regretted it, but I couldn't stop.

"He's already in the box! You're always saying that everything in the past goes in the box!"

Mum looked like someone had pressed the pause button on her face. She looked like she had lost her voice, expression, and even her breath.

I cursed myself from the bottom of my heart.

The piano-playing stops, and the next thing I know, Mum is standing in the kitchen. I smell coffee.

"Why don't you take a break?" Mum says as she pours the coffee with her right hand, a cigarette in her left. "It won't help to overwork yourself."

When I was living with the Professor, I learned how to cook for him. I made stewed dishes, pickled dishes, and even dried my own fish on the veranda. The Professor liked it when I did things like that.

I didn't wear any makeup. I didn't watch television. I didn't keep in touch with the few friends I'd had or with my family. I didn't leave the house aside from my daily walks and shopping in the neighbourhood. That was when I lived with the Professor, and before I met my true love.

The ocean in March has a calmness to it, lying far beyond Hull's windows. The regulars keep coming for lunch, and then for a drink or two at night before heading home.

"Do you want some coffee?" Sachiko asks, and I shake my head. I didn't want to create any opportunities for conversation. Ever since the incident involving Soko's high school plans, it's been awkward working at Hull. It's four p.m., and we have no customers.

"Soko's strong-willed," Sachiko says, even without the coffee. I respond with two or three short nods, but my reluctance to talk about it seems to be obvious and she chuckles.

"It's okay, I won't bite," she says. "That's a lovely skirt," she adds. "You kind of look like a stylish, modern nun."

I don't really know what a stylish, modern nun is like, but I humour Sachiko with a vague smile. The Professor had bought me the navy blue woollen skirt a long time ago. Sachiko is wearing a checked shirt again.

They're such kind people.

I go out to the backygarden to smoke. Sections of the grass are depressingly shrivelled, and a stack of empty boxes sits under the eaves. It's still light out, but the evening sky is turning slightly violet. I take a deep breath – I feel helpless.

I want to leave.

I want to leave. This restaurant. This city. This isn't where I belong.

It's been two years here now.

✦　✦　✦

"I'm thinking we should move," Mum says. "Of course, we'll wait until you graduate like I promised."

She's drinking coffee, her substitute for breakfast. Mum is pale in the mornings.

"Okay."

I don't panic one bit.

"I'll be moving into a dorm anyway. If I need to take an extra year to re-apply, I'll live and work at Hull."

Mum sighs.

"Soko." There's exhaustion in her face. It's not fair. It's not fair to look tired. "This isn't where we belong."

I put on a surprised look.

"Belong? We've never belonged anywhere."

We're birds of passage. And I'm sick of all this wandering.

"We *do* belong somewhere," Mum says. "I've told you before. Someday we'll be with your dad. He's where we belong."

Dad, again.

"That's crazy," I say, disgusted, and as usual, I regret my words as soon as they're out of my mouth. Trying hard to be nice to Mum, I correct myself. "It might be where you belong, Mum. But it's not where I do."

I want to face reality. Live in the real world.

"I have to go. I'll be late."

I'm in ninth grade, my last year in middle school. I have to turn in my high school choices by this summer.

We have a school assembly in the gym this morning. It feels good to walk through the hallway linking the old school building with the gym, with its close view of the nearby hills. I think green is a pretty colour.

"Look, it's Mr Sawada," Yoriko says.

He's walking alongside the parking lot, wearing his suede jacket that I've seen him wear many times. He doesn't come to morning assemblies because he only teaches at our school part-time.

"This is for you." At the beginning of the school year, he gave me a thin book, adding, "Don't tell anyone."

My heart skipped a beat. He'd apparently been to New York over spring break.

"They happened to be doing a Bonnard exhibit at the Museum of Modern Art."

It was a paperback book of Bonnard paintings.

"Thanks so much."

Mr Sawada smiled. I haven't told anyone about the book, naturally. Not even Mum or Yoriko. It's my secret.

The hallway is filled with students shuffling toward the gym.

I play the piano all morning. As long as I'm playing the piano, I can at least stay calm. I've been this way since I was a child. Whenever I was upset, I would play the piano. For hours and hours.

When my true love went away, I played the piano for an entire day. If I stopped, the tears flowed. The Professor just watched me play on and on. Silently, with an unreadable expression on his face.

I can't stop Soko.

I know that. Just like the Professor couldn't stop me.

"You've got big hands," my true love once said. "I love them," he told me, as he pressed his lips against the big, bony hands that I'd always kind of wanted to hide from men.

"I know how fast and powerfully these hands hit the piano keys, what beautiful music they create, and how they render the finest subtleties in sound."

We always held hands when we walked. My hands loved his.

Our little Soko.

"Soko, living in a dorm? Why are you so opposed?" he would surely say. "I think it's fine."

He would whisper softly it into my ear, holding me in his arms from behind. So that I wouldn't fall to pieces.

I knew from the beginning. That it was going to make me sad no matter what.

I'm about to go home after dinner at Hull when Mum says, "If you insist on living in a dorm, I guess it's okay."

She has a look of utter calm. I'm a bit surprised – though at the same time, I'm not surprised at all, but anyway – I ask, "Really?"

Mum doesn't answer my question. Instead, she says, "Good luck on your entrance exam."

Suddenly, I don't know what to say; I'm so taken aback. I'd grown so used to being defensive toward her.

"Thank you," is all I finally manage to say. Mum smiles quietly, but my heart fills with sadness instead of joy.

I knew this was how it would be. That it would make me sad regardless. It was the first time I'd ever disregarded Mum's input, and the first time she'd relented. More significantly, it was the first time I'd made a decision that I'd known would break her heart. I'm going to regret it. That's what I thought. No, that's not it. Maybe I'm already beginning to regret it. A dorm? Living a separate life? Is this what I want to do, no matter what? Now that Mum's come around, it's my turn to torment myself. A dorm? Living a life separate from Mum's? No matter what?

✦ ✦ ✦

Zushi is lush with nature. It's May, and there's an abundance of greenery just outside the window of this cheap white apartment.

I wake up and breakfast is ready, as it has been every day recently. Soko has early morning tutorials or something before school and leaves early. No matter how many times I tell her that I don't feel like eating in the morning, she tries to make me have something more than coffee for breakfast. Like eggs. Or vegetables. Today, she's peeled an apple. One piece is cut in the shape of rabbit ears.

I wonder where he is.

I light a cigarette, inhale slowly and deeply, and think. Where is he now, and what is he doing?

I might not make it.

The thought occurs to me. How am I supposed to go on living all alone, without him or Soko?

TOKYO, 2004

A rather sunny April morning marks a month since Soko left.

Life can really take a dark turn suddenly.

"It's not like someone died; it's a joyous occasion," Sachiko says, smiling, as if to console me. Of course to her, it may seem like a reason to celebrate.

"It's about time you let go of Soko and start thinking about your own happiness, Yoko."

I get fed up with my boss saying things like this to me. My happiness? I've already found it, and I've been happy ever since.

"Everything will be fine. Soko's a tough girl."

Even Mr Kono and Mr Wakatsuki offer the same ridiculous kinds of comments. Of course Soko is fine. She's bright and is unbelievably determined, just like my true love.

But…

I can't even fake a smile for the sake of the customers as I ponder silently.

Soko's not used to being alone.

Our little Soko. Soko, born in the middle of the night. Soko, my life's joy. As we walked to the crèche every day when in Takasaki, she would grow increasingly nervous, and cry when we arrived, without fail. Soko, who would always cling to my leg and not let go.

Ever since she left, the apartment has become deathly silent. It's lost colour and sound, and the air is motionless.

I don't have a reason to wake up in the morning, and I don't have a reason to eat or work. I go about my life half dead.

"Why don't you stay awhile after we close up tonight? We've got some good brandy," Sachiko says, but I politely decline. I don't intend on becoming a bellyaching drunk.

On Saturday two weeks ago, Soko came home for the night. Only two weeks had passed since she'd left, but she already seemed to have a different air about her. I asked for the day off from the restaurant, had dinner with Soko, and on Sunday morning we took a walk on the beach. But for some reason, we didn't have much to say.

"Any problems at school?" I asked.

"Not at all," Soko said casually.

Not at all! I was indignant, but then again, how else could she have responded?

I knew there were no problems. Soko had done a lot of research on her school, and we'd gone to look at the dorms beforehand. At her entrance ceremony, I watched Soko, who looked like any other high school girl amongst her fellow freshman, from far away – yes, far, far away, because parents are given no other choice. I introduced myself to her class teacher and guidance counsellor, and her dorm parent told me there was nothing to worry about. How absurd. What do they know?

It's May, and the leafy hydrangeas at Hisagi shrine are beginning to sprout tiny round flowers that are the same green hue as its leaves.

◆ ◆ ◆

Mum is calmer than I'd expected. During the two days I'm home, she says "Fine, then," about a dozen times.

"Have you made friends?"

"I don't know if you can call them friends, but there are people I talk to in my class."

"So you're having a good time?"

"Yeah."

"Fine, then."

"No problems?"

"Not at all."

"Really. Fine, then."

And so on.

Aside from a few questions, Mum is quiet. She smokes a lot of cigarettes like always – even when we say good-bye, all she says is "Take care," just like the day I moved into my dorm.

The day I moved into my dorm.

It was the saddest day of my life. Even though everything went smoothly. Even though I'm used to moving. Even though Mum and

I didn't exchange any sentimental words. It was a sunny, extremely depressing day that I had brought upon myself and that nobody could do anything about.

"Take care, then." Mum's voice had been so faint.

I'd passed the entrance exam, registered to attend the school, and graduated from middle school. Mum's boss and Sachiko-san threw a party for me, I packed, and by the day of my move, Mum and I had already resigned ourselves to the move – going through the motions without thought.

February, March, and April passed with nothing feeling real, the way time passes in a haze when you have a fever.

That's how I left home.

Maybe this was what it was like the day Mum left the Professor's house, too, I wondered. The sadness, the feeling of disbelief more than regret, but with part of you still composed in a strange way. There's no way to turn back now, so you just kept on forging ahead. As if so long as you keep forging ahead, you'll eventually wake from your dream and everything will be back to the way it was.

✦ ✦ ✦

It's raining.

The rain is beating down on the charcoal-grey surface of the ocean. It's two in the afternoon. Business is awfully slow today at Hull. Since morning, the owner has had the Beatles playing.

"He was going through some relationship problems when we met," Sachiko says. "I was giving him advice, and before we knew it, we were a couple."

I nod, but I don't understand why Sachiko is telling me this.

"The tomato chicken wasn't such a great hit, eh?" her husband shrugs as he rewrites the week's lunch menu. Then, glancing out the window, he says, "The rain isn't letting up at all, is it?"

I feel suffocated. The kinder they are, the more I want to leave.

Actually, I'd planned to move to a new city soon after Soko moved out. A new place. Anywhere, as long as I knew no one.

But as soon as Soko left, I lost the resolve even to move.

It's been three years and three months since I moved to Zushi. I've stayed in one place for too long. This isn't where I belong.

"We've never belonged anywhere."

I remember Soko's words and heave a sigh in my heart.

"This is reality."

I take the lunch plates out of the dish dryer and put them back on the shelves.

"I want to live in reality."

And Soko left. For a place where I'll never be able to reach her.

"I like this song," Sachiko says. It's a chilly day.

How did I believe that I would someday see him again? Now that Soko's gone, I feel that his existence itself was just a product of my imagination. Those eyes, that voice, those arms. Now that Soko's gone, there's nothing to prove that he once existed in this world, that he once loved me.

◆ ◆ ◆

It's been two months since I started high school. I've written Mum a letter every week, like I promised. I make an effort to write long letters, but Mum's responses are always painfully dry. Still, I feel a sense of relief when I see her handwriting—it's big and meticulous, and she always writes in blue ballpoint pen. From her letters I learn that the beach huts are being set up again for summer beachgoers, and that Mum put a silencer on the piano.

Living in a dorm means living with other people, and there's a set time for everything from meals to baths. I find that having to run into people wherever I go is a lot tougher than having to follow the countless rules, but life at school is pretty pleasant overall. Prep school is more peaceful than one might imagine. No one sticks their nose into other people's business.

I'm putting all my marbles into English, and I study it like mad. We have native English speaking teachers and the AV rooms and language labs are state-of-the-art and fun to use.

My room is at the end of the corridor on the second floor. The walls are cream-coloured, and it's small but has an air-conditioner.

Allie and the pink bear are in my closet. I haven't decorated the room, but I guess the art book by my bed kind of counts as decor. It's the Bonnard book that Mr Sawada gave me.

✦ ✦ ✦

I left Hull.

I'm still teaching piano, but I know I'm not a good teacher.

I put a silencer on the piano, so I can play in the middle of the night and early in the morning. That's really the only thing I've got these days.

"You can count on music," the Professor used to say.

"You can count on music, unlike human beings. It's always there. All you need to do is touch the keys. It'll appear right away. It'll materialize just like that, to whoever desires it."

Just like that, to whoever desires it.

I ask myself every morning under the covers, Why can't I just keep sleeping like this? Why can't I leave reality to Soko, and doze off for the rest of my life where my true love is, no matter how far away from the real world it is?

It feels like I'll be transported there, to where he is, to where I belong. If only I would stay asleep.

The dreams I have around dawn are always about him. But I'm not sure if they're my dreams or my imagination.

My walks have a different meaning for me now. When I'm walking alone, I feel as though I'm somewhere I've never been before. I think about how this place and I don't match. It's proof that I don't belong here.

Soko's favourites – the house with the lilies and the one with the dog – feel so foreign.

I've taken to having nightcaps. Every night before going to sleep, I drink a glass of wine. I can't sleep otherwise. I've decided to limit myself to one glass, though. Because I know it would break his heart if I were to become a drunk like some pathetic girl in an American novel.

I know it's foolish, but I still believe him.

✦ ✦ ✦

"School's almost out for the summer anyway, so there's no need for you to go out of your way to visit," Mum had said on the phone, but I decided to go home the next Saturday anyway. Sachiko-san had written me a letter saying that she was worried about Yoko. I knew from one of Mum's letters that she'd quit her job at Hull. She said that she'd quit because she was thinking of moving soon.

Whenever I ask, "How are you?" Mum always says that she's fine. Just like I do when she asks me.

The pay phones are located at one end of the dorm lounge. There's always someone on the phone with their family.

I did okay on my midterms. My grades weren't as great as they had been in the past, but I guess this is the best I can do for now.

I joined the art club again. The club has a clubroom separate from the regular art room for classes, but it's always messy and not very cosy. There's a really pretty upperclassman in the club.

Saturday, it's raining. I take several trains to get to Zushi. Whenever I come back here, I get this sort of sad, guilty feeling. I don't know why.

"Welcome home," Mum says at the door, as always. Mum never picks me up at the train station. "I just finished baking."

The apartment is filled with the sweet aroma of chocolate. Mum looks worn out. I never noticed it when I lived here, but now when I sometimes come home, I realize how small and battered the apartment is. The white, girly apartment.

"When are you moving?" I ask as I eat cake.

"I don't know yet," Mum says, and sips her dark coffee.

"Sachiko-san's worried about you," I say, and Mum lights a cigarette without any change in her expression. "Hm," is all she says.

"Where are you going to live next?" I ask, my voice awkwardly bright. Mum doesn't answer my question, and instead asks, "What do you want for dinner tonight?"

"Anything." With a heavy heart, I sip my café au lait.

❖ ❖ ❖

I sign Soko's overnight stay form for school and see her off on Sunday afternoon. I spend the rest of the afternoon playing the piano.

Soko grows more and more mature every time I see her. It was bound to happen. There's no way I could've kept her cooped up at home forever.

"This is reality."

Maybe Soko's words pointed to something that I'd been pretending not to see.

I'm tired, and I get under the covers without having dinner. As I drink a glass of wine, I open up a map and think about my move. Any place will do. I just need to get out of here soon.

I want to sleep in his arms.

Just one night. If I can sleep in his arms for just one night, I don't care if I die.

✦ ✦ ✦

"How are you?" I ask, before Mum does.

"Fine." I can sense that she has a faint smile on her face on the other end of the phone.

"Really?"

After a slight pause, Mum says, "Yes, that's what I said, isn't it?"

It's July. Mum feels farther and farther away. Even though I'm the one who left.

"I'll be home as soon as school's out for the summer."

Mum doesn't answer.

"Mum?"

I can tell she's lighting a cigarette she's put in her mouth.

"What did you have for dinner tonight?"

"Stuffed cabbage and minestrone."

A comedy program is playing on the television set in the dorm lounge. But the phones are far enough away, and plus, the volume is on low so I can hardly hear it.

"That sounds delicious."

"Not particularly."

I've been thinking about something for a long time. During class, art club, meals, all the time.

"Mum." I say. "Mum, should I come home?"

After a silence, Mum asks, "For the summer?"

But she knows what I mean.

"No." I stare at the blue linoleum floor and the slippers on my feet. Following what seems like a long pause, Mum sighs.

"Stop speaking nonsense."

"But," I begin.

Dismissively, she asks, "Are you homesick already? How pathetic." I remain silent.

"I can't believe it," Mum continues. "I can't believe that you're your father's daughter."

I don't respond.

"Come back for the summer. And then go back to school in the autumn. Do you understand?"

I don't know why, but I feel like crying.

"Do you understand?" Mum says one more time, and I tell her that I do.

"Good," Mum says airily, but there's still no energy in her voice.

When I go to Hull for the first time in a while, an orchestra of cicadas is in full song. I'm here to say good-bye.

"It'll be lonely around here," Sachiko says. "But you'll visit, right?"

She's wearing a checked shirt, like always.

"You still have to join us on our yacht," her husband says.

"Thank you."

It's cool inside the restaurant with the air-conditioning on. There's the counter, the cupboard, the refrigerator, the restaurant that looks so familiar to me.

Soon after the phone call from Soko, I'd decided where to move. I have no intention to live the "reality" that Soko speaks of, but I have absolutely no intention of running from it, either.

"So you're going back to Tokyo, huh?"

"Yes. It's been a while," I say as cheerfully as possible.

"How many years has it been?" Sachiko asks, and I tell her sixteen. Sixteen years.

"Let us know where you're living once you've settled in, okay?"

I smile once again and tell her I will.

✦ ✦ ✦

I received a matter-of-fact letter from Mum. I read it once and felt dazed. I read it again, reviewing what it said. It made my heart pound, which didn't stop for a while, but I wasn't surprised.

This is what it said:

Soko,

How are you doing? I've decided to move. This time, to Tokyo. I'll let you know as soon as I figure out where I'll be living, but I'll give you my parents' address and phone number. Spend the summer there. My parents − your grandparents − will be there. I've already told them about you. They're both alive. They're nice people, so please behave. Good luck on your final exams. I miss you. You're still my precious Soko.

Mum

So typical of Mum, I thought. All business. Even though she's talking about some crazy stuff, the letter is nonchalant.

The letter arrived yesterday, and my finals begin today. Tokyo. My grandparents. For the first time, I wish my exams would never end.

✦ ✦ ✦

Summers in Tokyo have a weird dryness to them. I remember it as soon as I get off the train. That, and the blueness of the summer sky in Tokyo.

For a while, I stand still on the platform.

It feels like nothing has changed. There are tons of people, and all I can see are buildings everywhere.

It makes me dizzy.

I was born here. I lived here. But quickly I realize that my absence has had no effect on the city. On the city's heartbeat.

Unexpectedly, my skin immediately recovers its memories of the place, and I can feel my arms, legs, and hair acclimate to the air.

I'm unbelievably nostalgic. Not emotionally. My mind and heart are frozen, but my body responds to the nostalgia all on its own.

Sixteen years? That can't be.

Closing my eyes, I breathe in the smell of the city. Everything feels like it had been a dream. Zushi, Takahagi, Kawagoe, Soka, Imaichi, everything. Even Soko's existence.

I wander over to an ashtray and light a cigarette. I catch a reflection of reality in a mirror on the platform. When I left everything and began wandering, I had been a mere twenty years old.

I don't go anywhere. I stay at a hotel near Tokyo station for the night. I have dinner by myself at a French restaurant in the hotel.

Returning to my room, I take a shower and call home.

"This is Yoko," I say.

My mother is silent for a moment – probably for as long as it takes to blink – and asks, "Where are you?"

Last week, when I'd called home for the first time in sixteen years, my mother was unable to speak through her tears, but she doesn't cry today. Rather, she sounds terrified and I feel like I've become a ghost.

"Tokyo."

"Where in Tokyo?"

A hotel, I tell her, and sit on the bed. I'd been talking to her standing up.

"Which hotel? Why won't you come home? Is Soko with you?"

I put a cigarette in my mouth and light it. I can't fully recall my mother's face.

"Yoko? Are you there? Don't hang up, I'm passing the phone to your dad."

My mother had had me when she was still fairly young, but she'd always looked old for her age. My cousin, Mihoko, used to say that it was because I was always causing her so much grief.

"Is that you, Yoko?"

My father's voice has a note of desperation. I have trouble remembering his face, too.

"Are you okay?"

"Yes," is all I can muster.

"Come home right away. Let bygones be bygones. It's okay."

It's okay. I don't know what's okay, but regardless, that's what he says.

"Dad, I told you last time, I can't go back there. And I'm sorry, but when Soko calls, will you let her stay..."

Of course, my father says.

"Of course. Don't worry about it. But why don't you come home, too."

"Dad."

I realize that I'm shaking.

"Regardless, just take care of Soko, please. I'll be in touch again."

Even after I hang up the phone, I continue to tremble for a while.

I meet them on the Odakyu line platform at Shinjuku station. By them, I mean Mum's parents. Just like we'd planned on the phone the day before, they're waiting at the very end of the platform. I can tell right away who they are, because they look like they're about to cry.

"Soko?" The lady says first. I know she's my grandmother, not just some lady, but anyway. "Look at you, all grown-up."

The lady cries. I feel like I'd done something bad, and want to apologise for Mum. Like, I'm sorry Mum was such a bad daughter.

Of course I can't, though. I'm nervous and don't know what to do.

The man doesn't say anything. He tries to carry my bag for me. I tell him that I can manage, but he takes it anyway and says, "Let's go." He says their car is parked in the parking lot of a department store.

"You were in Kurihira, I heard. You'd been so close all this time," the lady says, bursting into tears again.

The house Mum grew up in is in a place called Matsubara. It's a small, two-story house. On the piano in the drawing room, there are pictures of Mum and me as a baby. It feels weird. There's a new rice bowl and books there, just for me. The bowl is light pink with white plum blossoms. The books are a five-book set of Mary Norton's *The Borrowers* series.

"Let us know if there's anything you need. You're probably confused, too, suddenly having to spend the summer in a place like this."

According to the lady, I look exactly like Mum when she was a kid. She says she'll show me the photo albums the next day or the day after. And that Mum should be in touch with us soon.

That night, I sleep in Mum's room. I feel like our lives are slipping into this unfamiliar but stable place. I try to imagine Mum when she lived here, but I can't. Instead, I fall asleep remembering the Mum I do know. Mum's hands and face when she's playing the piano, the feel of her cheek pressed against mine when she embraces me, her smell, the way she walks with the hems of her flared skirt fluttering about, her skinny ankles, and her voice when she sings along to Rod Stewart on the Walkman.

In Mum's room, I can feel her. Just sort of, but tenderly.

✦ ✦ ✦

It's unbelievable how much Kitanomaru Park has remained unchanged since that day. The gates, the gentle slope, the dewy, raw scent of grass and trees. Even the women on their lunch break lounging on the benches of the observatory deck look exactly the same.

This is where my true love and I went our separate ways that day.

"I promise I'll be back."

It was a hot, humid evening. His eyes, voice, arms, everything was painfully sincere, leaving no room for doubt. The truth is always fleeting.

"Wherever you are, whatever you're doing, I swear I will find you again, Yoko."

Wherever I am. That's what he said.

I spoke to Soko on the phone last night.

"I met Mihoko. And Kaho, too," she said. "They told me stories about you when you were a kid."

She was speaking cheerfully because my father and mother were close by, but when I asked if she was comfortable there she was briefly at a loss for words. Then she asked, "When are you coming?"

I've forced her into what must be an awkward and helpless position.

"Soon," I said.

"I've already found an apartment. I'm going to go see the Professor tomorrow, and then I'll come get you. We'll go back to

Zushi first. We have to pack up our things and return the keys to the apartment.

Soko fell silent. Then she said, "You're going to see the Professor?" And then, "Will you be all right?"

I'll be fine, I assured her, but for now, in the middle of the day in Kitanomaru Park, I've been consumed by doubt.

There's a different nameplate at the apartment where we used to live. I walk over to the house nearby where the Professor's mother used to live, and the name there is the same as it was before. It's an old, small, Japanese-style house.

"Yes?"

The voice coming through the intercom is neither the Professor's nor his mother's. I barely stop myself from giving in to the urge to flee.

"This is Yoko Nojima. Is Professor Momoi in?"

I feel as though I might faint. How many times have I gone through these gates? There's a mandarin orange tree and a sink in the garden, and stacks of boxes on the veranda. Stepping stones line the way to the front door, and right outside the door is an umbrella stand.

"Just a moment, please."

Against my will, the memories come flooding back – fragments of my strange, but not unhappy, married life with the Professor – and my legs feel weak.

I hear the patter of sandals. The gate opens, and standing there is the Professor.

"Who would've thought."

The Professor has lost all his hair, but he's aged well.

"It's been a long time," I say, and bow respectfully.

"Who would've thought," the Professor says again.

In the western-style room at the front of the house, I am served the acidic coffee that the Professor likes. He introduces the thirty-something woman who brings the coffee as his wife. The Professor's mother apparently passed away ten years ago, and I pay my respects at the Buddhist altar in his house.

"So, how have you been? How's your child doing?"

The Professor calls Soko "your child." I don't know if it's out of consideration for his new wife or if he's forgotten Soko's name.

The windows are open, and though there's no wind, it's strangely cool inside.

"But really, who would've thought."

She'd been somewhat eccentric since she was a student, explains the Professor to his wife. Then he says, "As you know, we were once married, but one day she suddenly disappeared."

It was all I could do to smile. Sixteen years. I realize what a long time it's been.

I was hoping to be forgiven. I was hoping to see the Professor, and ask him for permission to return to Tokyo.

It's okay.

I remember my father's words as I drink the rest of my tart coffee.

"Oh, that fellow came by here a while ago. What was his name?" the Professor says in passing at the door, and my heart freezes as I put on my shoes.

"When?"

It's his wife who answers. "Over ten years ago. My mother-in-law was still with us then."

"He came for you, but I didn't know where you were."

Over ten years ago.

I close my eyes, and somehow stop the thoughts that come rushing. I shouldn't be thinking right now.

"I'm sorry to have visited without calling ahead."

I bow.

Over ten years ago. He'd come back. Here. For me. And then? Where did he go?

◆ ◆ ◆

Mum and I go back to Zushi.

Zushi brings back fond memories, with its perfect size and its convenience, the good food. We buy sashimi from the fishmonger by the train station. We also pick up red bean cakes at Nagashima.

Mum asks me just one question about her parents and childhood home.

"So, do you like them?" That's it.

"I don't know," I answer honestly.

Mum laughs and says, "That's only natural, huh? You've only just met them," and then, "You don't have to force yourself to get along with them."

We spend the entire summer packing slowly, little by little. Sometimes we pop by Hull for a meal or some tea.

On sunny days, we take walks on the beach.

During the day, Mum often slacks off from packing to play the piano. Once, she cries as she plays.

"I was just thinking about how tough life is," she says, when I ask her later that night why she'd been crying. She looks sad, but has a smile on her face.

"But we've got to keep ploughing forward," I say, and Mum answers, "Exactly." Looking sad, but still smiling.

I return to my dorm at the end of August.

As soon as I get back, I write Mum a letter. This is what I says:

Dear Mum,

How are you? Summer was fun, wasn't it? I'm glad that you're going back to Tokyo. Everyone there was really nice to me.

I hope you can start a new life now. You're beautiful, so maybe you'll even find yourself a boyfriend.

I'll be back when school is on holiday. Take care.

Soko

P.S. You are my treasure.

❖ ❖ ❖

That's how I found myself back in Tokyo.

Still without a clue why I wake up in the morning, why I eat, or why I work, I continue to live just so that I can see him one more time. It might upset Soko and sadden him, but there's nothing I can do about it.

As for work, I'm waitressing at a traditional Japanese restaurant and playing the piano at a cheap steakhouse. What's surprised me most since I've been back to Tokyo is how expensive rent is.

I don't care if I die any day now. I really don't.

On my days off, I sometimes drop by my parents' house. What remains there is not my past, but someone else's memories. My father's. Or my mother's. Or the person I was, who died long ago.

I usually spend my nights drinking. It's almost a miracle that the bar is still there. The place where I used to drink Sicilian Kisses with my true love. The place where it all began.

I only play the piano at work, and I can no longer listen to Rod Stewart. In this city, the things that used to cheer me feel like mere artifice. Music is no longer my ally, and Soko has gone far away.

It may be closer to the truth to say that I want to die soon, rather than that I don't care if I die any day now.

When I work at the restaurant, I wear a kimono.

✦ ✦ ✦

I get a lot of packages from Mum's parents. They're filled with books, red bean sweets, and fruit.

In addition to the art club, I've become a member of the English debate club. The pretty girl in the art club is in eleventh grade, and her name is Shindo-san. Mum never picks up when I call her at night. When I call her in the morning on her days off, she sounds like she's just come back from the dead.

"Mum?" I say first.

Then she asks, "How are you?"

But when I ask her the same thing and she says she's fine, nothing in her voice lets me believe her.

"Sports day's coming up at school. Do you want to come watch?" I'd asked during our latest conversation.

"Yeah, probably."

Mum's reaction wasn't like her at all, and for some reason I'm scared stiff.

✦ ✦ ✦

Death is here, as something peaceful. Always.

I think about this every night as I drink my gin and tonic.

"When we die, we'll no doubt turn into water," my true love often said after bone-melting sex so wonderful that it felt as though the skin between my body and his was nonexistent. "We'll turn into water and wash away as we hold each other like this."

"Like a river?"

"Right. Like a river."

"As we hold each other?"

"Yes. We'll never part."

With our arms and legs entwined. Like a river.

It seemed so simple. It seemed so simple and so right, so utterly safe.

"When we die…"

In the dim light, the gin and tonic in my glass looks like a river at night. A clear river flowing through the depths of a forest.

"When we die…"

When the door opens, there's no need for me to turn around.

It's dark and crowded in the bar, and there's music. Footsteps and all other signs of movement are drowned out. What I feel is something much stronger and more tangible than any of that, like a sudden change in temperature or the pressure of a solid presence.

I know it's him.

I'm sure it's him as naturally as if we'd just seen each other yesterday, spent the day working in separate places, and met up again today like we'd promised.

I can't tell whether I'm incredulous or whether I expected it.

He approaches slowly, stands behind me, and touches my right cheek gently with his right hand.

"It's been a while." His voice is the same gentle, sweet voice that makes me weak and that I've missed so much.

I lean my head to the right just slightly to make sure his fingers are real. No emotions accompany the action. I can't even look at his face.

"I can't believe it," I whisper, realizing only as I say it that that's what I'm thinking.

"I can't either," he says, and we both discover our voices quivering. The realization hits us at the same time, and the realization that we've realized this hits us at the same time as well. This is the how it always is. I don't know why, but it is.

It might take a year to find the words. It might take another year to feel safe to cry, and probably another year to turn around and put my arms around him.

Before I know it, though, my right hand is firmly enveloped in a warm hand on his left knee. He's sitting next to me. Like always.

EPILOGUE

We Didn't Mean to Go to Sea.

This is the title of a novel by Arthur Ransome. In life, we can sometimes find ourselves in such situations. Yoko was probably severed from her previous existence in the same way.

I didn't mean to go to sea.

That's how it feels when one falls in love.

Yoko, with her daughter, has been travelling for many years. This is a tale of a wandering mother and daughter. And what a story.

But if the journey is indeed on God's Boat, it shouldn't be moored anywhere. That's what I thought. So I undid the rope. No matter where the boat might drift to.

It all began at a bar. If I hadn't had that golden cocktail, sweet enough to knock anyone out, this novel never would have been written.

I enjoyed visiting the many cities I researched for this book.

While it is simple and quiet, the tale is one of madness. Even now, I believe it to be the most perilous novel I've written thus far.

Kaori Ekuni
Early summer, 1999